The
Black Knight

by

FLORA KIDD

Harlequin Books

TORONTO • LONDON • NEW YORK • AMSTERDAM • SYDNEY • WINNIPEG

Original hardcover edition published in 1976
by Mills & Boon Limited

ISBN 0-373-02056-2

Harlequin edition published March 1977

Printed in Canada

For Edna, who is as fascinated by
archaeology as I am

CHAPTER ONE

THE bus trundled over a bridge that spanned a narrow river. Sandy Phillips peered through the window and saw a signpost at the side of the road. One word was painted on it—Scotland.

Excitement leapt within her. At last she had crossed the border and was in that part of Great Britain which she had never visited before; that country of moorland and mountain, of deep green glens and broad blue lochs, of castles and crofts.

Hundreds of years ago Roman soldiers had marched this way and had been absorbed into a misty wilderness. It wasn't surprising that one of their legions had been lost, thought Sandy, as she gazed out at the fine drizzling rain which rolled cloud-like across grey-green sodden fields and hid any view there might have been of distant hills.

Maybe the same would happen to her. Maybe she would be sucked into the mist as she was tempted to see what lay behind it, and, like the soldiers of old, she would be lost for ever.

Amused by her tendency to indulge in historical daydreams, she gave her head a shake and returned to reality. The bus had swerved on to a road which forked left. Another signpost reared up at the wayside. Gretna Green. The words spelt high romance, for it had been here at the old village smithy that so many eloping couples had been married in times gone by.

The bus stopped. Some passengers got off and new ones took their places. The bus continued on its way, passing neat whitewashed council houses and small detached bungalows, until once again it was in the open countryside where scattered farmhouses were surrounded by fields, dim and desolate in the wan light of the wet summer evening.

The first and longest part of Sandy's journey that day, from London to Carlisle, had been fast and comfortable in the long-distance bus which had swept along at a steady speed, making few stops. By comparison this part of the journey, which was taking her into the part of Scotland known as Galloway, had so far been slow and bumpy. Many times the vehicle left the main road and meandered down a country lane to a village to pick up passengers before wandering back to the main road.

But Sandy was too excited to be put off by discomfort. Although she had been travelling since early that morning she sat upright, her square shoulders straight and her grey eyes bright and alert.

She was a tall slim girl with long legs which were at present clothed in faded blue jeans. Over a thin cotton turtle-necked jumper she wore a blue anorak. Her hair hung straight from a central parting to her shoulders, and it was the colour of pale sand.

Nearly two months ago she had graduated from a university with a degree in History. Three years of study had been crowned with success. Since then she had been occupying herself with various jobs in the town where she lived with her parents, hoping to make some money to enable her to return to university to take a further degree.

And then out of the blue the letter had come from her cousin Martha. She had read it eagerly, hopefully, for Martha, lovable impulsive Martha, who had been widowed so suddenly and tragically by the death of her husband, Crawford Caldwell, in a car-racing accident, had said she would write from her husband's ancestral home in Scotland and would invite Sandy to stay with her if she found her father-in-law agreeable to the arrangement.

Opening her leather satchel-like handbag, Sandy found the letter, took it out and read it over again.

8

'Dearest Sandy,

As you'll see by the address I arrived safely at Duncreggan, but oh, what a shock I received. Crawford's father died nearly two years ago and we didn't know! Apparently efforts were made to contact Crawford at the time, but all letters were returned from the addresses to which they were sent. That was the price Crawford paid for always being on the move.

The place now belongs to Lymond, Crawford's twin brother. There is an old castle, but we don't live in it. We live in the New House, as it's called, which isn't very new any more, being about two hundred years old. You would love it here. It's full of historical associations.

Lymond has invited me to stay and I've accepted the invitation. I see by the date I've been here almost six weeks! I've decided that for Dermid's sake I must stay and make my home here. It was Crawford's home once and he wanted his son to grow up here and have the same advantages as he had, so I must stay.

But oh, Sandy dear, I feel in need of moral support, the kind only a member of one's own family can give. You're the nearest to a sister I'll ever have, and I'm wondering if you have a job for the rest of the summer. If you haven't, please come here. In return for your keep you could look after Dermid for me for a few hours a day. He's behaving badly and I don't seem able to cope with him. When I remember how good you were with him the short time he and I stayed with Aunty Jane, Uncle Tom and you when I returned to England, I feel sure your presence here for the summer would help him to settle in.

Everyone here has been very kind and welcoming and I've made some new friends. However, I find Lymond a little aloof and puzzling.

Please, Sandy, come. It would help me enormously to have you here, someone of my own in whom I can confide until Dermid and I are established here. If you can come let me know how and where you are arriving and I'll arrange for you to be met.

'Martha.'

Sandy folded the letter up, returned it to its envelope and put it back in her handbag. When she had received it she had shown it to her mother, Martha's Aunty Jane, who had said immediately,

'You must go. You know what Martha's like. She knows what she should do, but has difficulty in carrying out her intentions. She wants to stay there for the boy's sake, which is good, but reading between the lines I'd say she's afraid of her brother-in-law. Go and stay with her, Sandy. Hold her hand and encourage her. That's all she's ever needed, someone to love her and give her a sense of security . . .'

So arrangements had been made for Sandy to travel the cheapest way she could, and now here she was on a country bus entering the town of Annan.

The bus stopped in the wide rain-swept main street and there was a flurry of movement and the soft sing-song of Scottish voices as more people got on the bus. A woman sat down beside Sandy, excusing herself humorously for taking up so much room on the seat. She had a big bunch of roses in her hand, and when Sandy admired them she explained that she was going to the hospital at Dumfries to see her daughter who had just had her first baby.

'I can tell by the way ye speak ye're not from around here yerself,' she added, giving Sandy a curious but friendly glance.

'No, I'm from Hampshire, in the south of England. I'm on my way to Duncreggan Castle.'

'Och, now whatever would ye be wanting to go to that old place for?'

'To stay with my cousin. She's living there just now. Do you know it?'

10

'Aye, I do that. I was born not far away and my brother still has a farm near there, where I grew up.'

'Then you'll know something about the family who own the castle.'

'The Black Caldwells, ye mean?' The woman chuckled. 'Aye, there isn't much I don't know about them.'

'Why are they called black?'

'It's because of their colouring, ye ken. They have awful black hair and sometimes their eyes are black, but it could be because of their black deeds in the past.' Again the woman chuckled.

'What sort of black deeds?'

'Och, they were a wild lot. If they weren't smuggling they were reiving . . .'

'Reiving? Whatever was that?'

'It's an old word meaning stealing. They used to take other people's cattle and sheep. Mind you, they weren't the only ones who did that in these parts. They were just better at it than anyone else. But with time they became respectable and wealthy, although I've heard that Major Sir Gavin Caldwell, who died a couple of years ago, didn't leave a penny. He did well in the army, like many a Caldwell before him, and he won medals for bravery in action. But he kept very much to himself after his wife died. Aye, and that was a sad affair. She was a minx, so she was, and she left him with two sons to bring up, as wild a pair of scamps as you'd find anywhere, living up to the Caldwell reputation for mischief. The eldest one is living at the castle now. Och, and it doesn't seem like twelve years since he left home with a flea in his ear from his father for behaving badly and disgracing the family. They do say he's a bit dour, now.'

The conversation passed to other subjects. The bus entered the outskirts of a town. It stopped and the friendly garrulous woman departed. As the bus lurched on along the wet streets Sandy had an impression of red sandstone buildings, dark with rain, a glimpse of an old clock tower standing in the middle of what seemed to be the main street, and then the bus was sweeping down to a wide esplanade beside a river where other buses were parked or were just leaving.

As she stepped down on to the wet roadway, soft damp air touched her cheeks and misted her hair. For a moment she stood listening to the sound of the river as it rushed over a weir, wondering whether Martha had come to meet her.

'Miss Phillips?'

The voice spoke behind her. It was masculine, cool and indifferent, as if its owner didn't really care whether she was Miss Phillips or not.

Sandy turned. The man standing behind her was only a little taller than herself. He had broad shoulders slanting under a short yellow waterproof jacket which glistened with raindrops. His wet hair was black, roughly cut so that it curved across his forehead and round his ears. Above the turned-up collar of the jacket his face was taut and tough, and no smile softened its hard, finely-chiselled features nor twinkled in the depths of his deep-set dark eyes.

'Yes, I'm Sandy Phillips,' she replied with a smile. 'Who are you?'

'Caldwell of Duncreggan.'

Umpteenth of that ilk, thought Sandy to herself flippantly, in the way of genealogical lists which show the descent of a family. He must be Lymond, the aloof and puzzling one, who had inherited the Caldwell estate.

'Is that all your luggage?' he asked, pointing to her rucksack.

'Yes. I travel light,' she said, trying another smile, refusing to be put off by his autocratic manner.

'The young usually do,' he remarked drily, and at once she felt dismissed as someone who was beneath his notice. 'The car is parked on the other side of the street. This way.'

He picked up the rucksack effortlessly, turned on his heel

and strode away. Sandy followed him across the wide wet roadway to a rather battered-looking car. She hoped to see Martha and Dermid sitting in it, waiting to welcome her, but it was apparently empty. Caldwell of Duncreggan unlocked the boot, placed her rucksack in it on top of a motley collection of tools, and slammed it shut.

'Get in,' he ordered as he made his way round to the door on the driver's side of the car.

'Front or back seat?' she asked politely.

'Please yourself. Both doors are unlocked,' he answered carelessly, and she felt the first stirring of resentment. She did not expect any special treatment because she was a woman, but she was finding his indifference a little galling.

Since there seemed to be something on the back seat, under a sack, she opened the front door and slid into the seat just as the driver, who had already seated himself, turned on the ignition. He had removed his waterproof jacket and had thrown it on the back seat, and now she could see he was wearing a safari-style jacket of some fine grey material over a black high-necked sweater.

He revved the engine, released the brake, shifted the gear lever, and the car jerked forward reluctantly. Down the road they went to turn left over a bridge and chug up an incline to some traffic lights, where they stopped. Sandy stared at the signpost. Glasgow to the right, several other towns straight on. The lights changed and the car jerked forward and continued ahead.

The windscreen wipers made an irritating creaking noise as if they needed oiling. The engine, too, was noisy as if there were a hole in the silencer. Sandy wasn't quite sure what she had expected, but it certainly wasn't such a battered vehicle. Martha had always given the impression that Crawford's family were fairly wealthy and able to afford super sports cars and limousines.

Then there was the smell. It was all-pervading. She looked round cautiously. A quick glance at the sacking on

13

the back seat made her eyes open wide. She blinked and looked again. A small pig was lying on the seat under the sack. Only its head was showing. Its eyes were closed. She hoped it wasn't dead.

Satisfied because she had found the cause of the smell, Sandy looked out of the window. There were houses, old ones, sturdy and solidly built of red sandstone, screened by dark shrubs, rhododendron and laurel. The houses gave way to modern bungalows. Here and there lights glimmered in the slow-creeping dusk which had come early because of the rain.

Then there were fields rolling away to a thick grey distance, dotted with clumps of trees, stiff dark pines mingling with the softer, more rounded outlines of ash and elm, looking sad as they dripped with moisture. The road curved in a long bend beside a stone wall which was over-hung by tall elegant beech trees. A gateway appeared and Sandy had a glimpse of a straight driveway leading up to a big grey house before the road twisted again round another bend.

She felt questions bubbling up inside her. Several times she thought of asking them, only to be put off by the wall of silence which Lymond Caldwell had built around himself.

Furtively she glanced at him, remembering the description given of him by the woman on the bus, Dour, an old Scots word from the Latin word *durus*, meaning hard. Yes, he looked hard, and his profile, straight forehead, aquiline nose, high cheekbones, thin straight mouth and angular jaw, looked as if it had been carved from some hard stone. In fact he resembled very closely the carving of a Norman knight on an old tombstone in the church near her home in Hampshire.

Carried away once again on one of her historical fancies, Sandy looked out of the window. The first Caldwell to come to Scotland could have been a Norman knight, she imagined, one of those who had come north from England to help David the First stabilise the Scottish kingdom and in return had received grants of land.

Pleased with her theory, she turned again to the man, thinking to ask him whether it was correct, and was again silenced by his attitude of superior indifference. She might as well not be there for all the notice he was taking.

A Black Caldwell. Perhaps that knight of old had worn black armour on the field of battle. A black knight, capable of black deeds and yet capable of bravery too, the stuff of which war heroes are made.

The road was climbing a hill. It forged straight as an arrow between dark trees, like a Roman road. Headlights were necessary now and they glared through the murk from cars passing the other way.

'How long will it take us to reach Duncreggan Castle?' asked Sandy. The silence was breached at last. It was a question he would have to answer.

'Another hour.'

A man of few words, obviously, thought Sandy to herself with a little grin as she slumped down in the seat so as to be more comfortable and rest her head against the back of it.

'Is there a town near it?' she persisted.

'Kirkton.'

'Is it big?'

'No. About five thousand people. Maybe less.'

'Could I have got to Kirkton from Dumfries by bus?' she asked.

'You could.'

Like drawing blood from a stone, thought Sandy, grinning to herself again, but she wasn't going to be put off. She could not spend an hour with a person in such confined quarters without speaking.

'Then you shouldn't have gone to the trouble of going to Dumfries to meet me,' she said. 'I could have got the bus.

I'm very good at finding my own way to places.'

Again there was silence and she thought he was not going to react. He reached down a hand to change gear because the engine was protesting against the long haul up the gradual hill, then cursed briefly as a car going in the opposite direction flung spray all over the windscreen in a muddy splatter.

'I didn't go to any trouble,' he said quietly. 'I had to go into Dumfries today. Martha told me you would be arriving at the Whitesands terminus this evening, so I offered to meet you.'

'Oh. Thank you. That was kind of you.'

'No, you've got it all wrong,' he jibed softly. 'I don't do anything to be kind, but because it's convenient. If you'd taken the bus to Kirkton you'd have arrived there at eleven-thirty tonight and either Johnnie or I would have had to turn out to meet you. It's better and quicker this way.'

More silence. The car reached the top of the hill and dipped down the other side. The road began to wander again, winding round fields and through small clusters of cottages. The rain seemed to come down more thickly, and to seep through the narrow gaps where the doors of the car closed, making everything feel damp.

Sandy stared out at the darkening countryside. There was no doubt in her mind now that Lymond Caldwell did not want her at Duncreggan. Perhaps Martha had invited her without consulting him first. The thought rattled around in her mind, making her frown uneasily. It would be just like her impetuous, frivolous cousin to do that, never thinking that she might place not only Sandy in an embarrassing position but also her host.

'I hope it's all right for me to stay with Martha at Duncreggan for the rest of the summer,' she said tentatively.

He reacted immediately, turning his head sharply and

16

giving her a quick glance from narrowed eyes. Then he turned his attention to the road again, because it was slippery.

'I wondered how long you'd be staying,' he said. 'I wondered also why you've come at all. Did Martha invite you?'

So her guess had been right, not that knowing it made her feel any better. In fact she felt more than embarrassed. She felt mortified.

'Yes, she did,' she replied in a small voice. 'Didn't she tell you?'

'All she said this morning, when she heard that I had to drive to Dumfries, was that a relative of hers was arriving and would like to see the Castle. I got the impression you were passing through on your way to somewhere else and would stay one night.'

Sandy was stunned. Why hadn't Martha told him the truth? She glanced at his hard uncommunicative profile and guessed why. Martha had been afraid that Lymond Caldwell would have refused to let her cousin stay for the rest of the summer, if she had asked him.

'She wrote and asked me to come and help her with Dermid,' she began, feeling that some explanation was necessary.

'Is that what you do for a living?' he asked, cutting in rather rudely, she thought. 'Are you a children's nanny?'

'No. It's just a summer job, while I'm on vacation from university.'

He gave her another narrowed glance through the gloom which was now thickening almost to darkness in the car.

'I hope you're not expecting to be paid,' he said sharply.

'Oh, no. Martha said I'd get my keep for helping her with Dermid,' she explained diffidently. There was nothing worse, she thought, than being at a disadvantage when dealing with someone like Lymond Caldwell, who behaved with a natural arrogance which he had probably inherited from the feudal lords who had been his ancestors.

'Look, Mr Caldwell,' she said, turning to him appealingly. 'I feel very badly about this. Martha should have asked you first.'

'You're damned right, she should,' he grated. 'But over the past few weeks I've discovered she's anything but straightforward. And I can't understand why she needs help in looking after the child. She's nothing else to do but look after him.'

'Well, most women make better mothers if they can have a short time to themselves each day, and I should think that Martha, more than most women, finds motherhood trying and tying ...' Sandy found she was groping for an explanation because, truth to tell, she had never before given any serious consideration to the human condition known as motherhood—for the simple reason that it was a condition in which she did not expect to find herself for years.

'Why do you say more than most women?' he asked. 'Why should Martha resent being a mother more than other women?'

'I don't think she *resents* it. I think she finds it difficult because she's still quite young ...'

'I've known younger mothers,' he interrupted her drily.

'And she's an only parent ...'

'You think that's new?' he cut in again.

'I'm only trying to explain how I think Martha is feeling,' she countered a little huffily, irritated by his quick sharp retorts. 'She's always had a great zest for life ...'

'You mean for having a good time, regardless of who else suffers,' he jibed. 'Then she and Crawford must have made a great pair. But you'd think his death would have had some effect on her and made her simmer down a bit.'

'I suppose you expect her to go around in sackcloth and ashes for the rest of her life just because she's been widowed, mourning for what might have been,' she retorted spiritedly. Perhaps he was one of those puritanical Scots she had read about who didn't believe in having a good time.

He laughed, a rather sardonic sound, but she couldn't see his face clearly any more because the gloom had deepened both inside and outside the car as dusk gave way to night.

'No, I don't expect that,' he replied coolly. 'When did you see her last?'

'When she returned to England after the accident. She was very shaken up. In fact it was some time before we could get her to go out and face the world. Mother, who has always looked after Martha ever since her own parents were killed, wanted her to stay longer, but Martha was determined to come to Scotland because she had promised Crawford that if anything ever happened to him on the race-track she would take Dermid to see your father. She had no idea he had died.'

'Humph. So I gathered,' he growled. 'And I had no idea that Crawford had a wife and child until they both landed on my doorstep a few weeks ago. It had never crossed her mind, apparently, to write and ask if she could come to Duncreggan.'

Sandy flinched from the implied criticism of Martha's lack of manners and sat for a few minutes in silence, nibbling at her lower lip.

'Why didn't you know about her and Dermid? Didn't you keep in touch with your brother?'

'I tried over the years, but soon got tired of not receiving answers to my letters or having them returned with the words "moved—address unknown" written across them. I wrote to him when the old man died, but he didn't reply.'

'But what about your father? Didn't your brother write to him?'

Again he laughed. 'No,' he said.

19

'Why not?'

'Ever heard of pride, Miss Phillips? Well, the Caldwells have always had more than is good for them, and my father and Crawford had a superabundance of it. Once Crawford did something to offend my father, who told him to clear out and never come back. Being Crawford he did just that—and didn't even soften sufficiently to write and tell the old man he had a grandson.'

'Oh, how vindictive! How positively medieval!' exclaimed Sandy, who coming from a close-knit family, the members of which had always kept in touch, found such behaviour extremely uncivilised.

'I agree with you. I'd even go one step further and say it was positively barbaric,' he said with a chuckle, 'but then the Caldwells have never been noted for gentle qualities. And I suspect that if Martha had known the truth about us, she wouldn't have turned up as she did. She was slightly shocked when I told her that instead of leaving a will, which might have divided the estate equally between his two sons, my father died intestate and left an accumulation of debts which I'm still trying to pay off.'

'But if he didn't leave a will, how were you able to inherit the estate?' she asked.

'It was entailed to go to the eldest son. And I was the elder of the two of us, by about five minutes,' he replied drily.

'So there was nothing for Crawford?'

'Nothing was left to him. There are some old cars which he collected when he used to live at Duncreggan.' He gave another derisive chuckle. 'You should have seen your cousin's face when I showed them to her and when I told her that the roof of the house leaks when there's a bad storm. I'm surprised she's stayed as long as she has, considering the uncomfortable circumstances in which she finds herself living just now.'

Again Sandy sat in stunned silence, recalling the letter in

her handbag. 'For Dermid's sake I must stay and make my home here. It was Crawford's home once and he would have wanted his son to grow up here and have the same advantages as he had, so I must stay,' Martha had written.

How could she stay when she was so obviously not welcome? How could she impose upon this man who was struggling to pay off his father's debts while his roof leaked? What advantage was there for Dermid in living in such a place? Surely it would be better if Martha returned to the south where she could get work, where she could leave Dermid to be looked after by Sandy's mother.

'Mr Caldwell, I feel I must apologise for Martha. She shouldn't impose upon your hospitality. She told me you had invited her to stay.'

'I did. Dermid is my brother's son. I thought I ought to get to know him.' He broke off and she heard his breath hiss in a sigh of exasperation.

'Are you getting to know him?' she asked.

'Not very well,' he replied tautly.

'I think I understand now why you're not exactly welcoming,' said Sandy slowly. 'I won't stay. I'll go back tomorrow, that is if you'll let me stay the night.'

He made no reply to that and, feeling suddenly drained of all energy, Sandy subsided into a troubled silence, once more staring out of the window.

They were approaching a town. Lights were twinkling from windows. Rows of lights curved up dim hillsides, showing where there were roads. The car slowed down and took a left turn. A church steeple loomed on the right and then there were shops with blank plate-glass windows which reflected the car as it passed by. Apart from a few youths hanging round the entrance of a well-lit chip shop, the main street was deserted on that wet night.

Soon they were in the country again. Trees made a tunnel that dripped on the roof of the car. The tunnel ended and the road meandered over open land. Strange shapes, with glimpses of opal eyes, appeared in front of the car. Lymond slowed down and touched the horn. The shapes shambled away.

'What were they?' asked Sandy.

'Sheep. Must be a fence down,' was the terse answer.

In the back seat the little pig, disturbed by the sound of the horn, grunted and snuffled. Sandy felt her head dip and nod. Jerking it upright, she stared straight ahead, willing herself to stay awake, but in spite of her efforts her eyes closed and she dozed.

It was the sound of gears changing down which brought her back from her uneasy doze, and she opened her eyes to see two tall gateposts of weather-worn stone, mottled with lichen and glistening with raindrops in the twin shafts of light from the headlights. No gate hung between them, and the driveway beyond them was rutted mud and gravel over which the car bumped and jerked.

The driveway curved to the right. A house loomed out of the darkness. The car was stopped at the bottom of a flight of shallow steps which led up to a wide porch supported on pillars of stone. Under the porch was an elegantly-panelled door with a spider's-web fanlight above it.

Lymond turned off the engine, switched off the lights and reached into the back for his yellow jacket. He opened his door, got out, shrugged into his jacket and went to the back of the car to open the boot.

Sandy pulled on the hood of her anorak to keep her hair dry, opened her door and got out and also went round to the back of the car. She took out her rucksack and Lymond closed the boot.

'Go into the house,' he ordered in his cool casual way. 'I have to take the pig to the sty.'

Obediently Sandy humped her rucksack up the steps to the front door. By the rather poor light given out by the two lanterns on either side of the door she could see that the black paint was peeling off the panelling.

Beside the door was an old-fashioned brass bell-pull. She grasped it and pulled. To her shock and surprise it came away in her hand, leaving a gaping hole. It was unattached to any wires which might have set a bell ringing inside the house.

Her surprise giving way to rueful amusement, Sandy tried to put the bell-pull back in its place, but it wouldn't stay in and fell with a clang on to the step. She picked it up and was wondering what to do with it when she heard footsteps crunching on the gravel. In a few seconds Lymond appeared. He sprang up the steps, his glance going to the bell-pull in her hand.

'I tried to ring the bell and this fell out,' she explained, holding it out to him.

'I hope you're not one of those unfortunate people who destroy everything they touch,' he mocked, taking it from her and deftly putting it back in its place, where it stayed. 'Because if you are, Duncreggan House is certainly not for you. Most of its contents fall to pieces if not handled with care. All you had to do was turn the door knob. The door is never locked.'

He opened the door and signalled to her to step inside. She entered the house slowly and found herself in a wide hallway. A chandelier hung from the beautiful central moulding of the ceiling, but not all of its sockets carried light bulbs, so that the light it shed was very dim.

A faded, threadbare square of Indian carpet covered the centre of the parquet floor, but the flight of stairs going up to the right was uncarpeted. A few antique chairs with tapestry seats were set about the hall, and several huge paintings in gilt frames hung on the pale walls.

A door to the right opened and a woman came out of a room from which came the sound of a television set. Sandy had hoped to see Martha, but the woman was taller and older than her cousin.

'I thought I heard the door,' she said in a soft sing-song voice. 'Did you find the girl from England, Lymond?'

'I did,' he replied. 'This is she, Sandy Phillips.'

'Welcome to Duncreggan,' said the woman, with a faint sweet smile. Her grey-sprinkled dark hair was wound round her head in braids and she was wearing a sagging tweed skirt and a thin woollen jumper.

'This is Nan Currie,' said Lymond briskly to Sandy. 'She's kept house here for nearly twenty years.'

'Aye, that's so.'

'Where's Martha?' asked Lymond.

'She went down to the yacht club with Johnnie.'

'And the child?'

'Asleep, after many, many stories.' Again the woman smiled gently to herself. Then turning to Sandy she said, 'I expect you're tired after that long journey and could do with a bite to eat. I'll away to put the kettle on. Put your rucksack at the foot of the stairs ready to take up to your room. You'll find a wee cloakroom through that door on the left where you can wash your hands. Then come to the kitchen. We don't use the dining room much these days.'

Relieved to find a normal welcome after all, Sandy dutifully washed her hands and found her way to the kitchen along a passage which went off to the right from the hall. Sitting at a big table set with a bright, checked tablecloth, she ate the meal set before her hungrily and silently, aware that Lymond was doing the same.

The kitchen was big and square and had a stone floor. A fire leapt in the old-fashioned grate, a welcome sight on that dreary wet night, and its flickering flames were reflected in the copper kitchen utensils which hung on the walls. Someone had tried to make the place brighter by painting the cupboards gaudy yellow, and there were many indoor plants crowded on shelves and sideboards.

Nan waited on them, pouring hot dark tea from a huge brown earthenware teapot, occasionally asking Lymond a question about his visit to Dumfries and listening to his answer with her head tipped slightly to one side as she watched Sandy.

Looking up and finding that grave dark glance fixed on her, Sandy was struck suddenly by certain resemblances between the woman and Lymond. Nan's hair, it was true, was streaked with grey, but once it had been as jet black as Lymond's was now. They both had very dark, almost black, eyes. Their skin had a similar ivory tint which gave them both a foreign look as if, long ago, some ancestor had come from the eastern Mediterranean.

She could be his mother, with that colouring, thought Sandy, and the thought had hardly passed through her mind when Nan spoke softly:

'No, not his mother, but his father's first cousin. Gavin Caldwell and I shared grandparents, and my mother was his father's sister.'

'Oh!' exclaimed Sandy, her grey eyes flashing as she looked away from Lymond and back at Nan. 'How did you know what I was thinking?'

'You are young and your eyes are clear, mirroring your thoughts,' replied Nan, and now her voice held a sonorous quality and her dark eyes looked past Sandy. 'You have not yet learned to hide them. You are as open as the day, which makes you a nice person, but is dangerous for you.'

'Are you at it again?' Lymond was gently scoffing. He turned to Sandy and explained. 'Once a Caldwell married a gypsy lass. She was supposedly the daughter of the king of the local gypsies. Nan doesn't half play up that little smattering of gypsy blood in her veins, pretending she can read your mind and even foretell the future. You should take any prediction she makes with a grain of salt.'

'You shouldn't make fun of what is your heritage as well as mine,' Nan chided him, although her smile was affectionate.

Yes, the gypsy blood might account for their dark

colouring, thought Sandy, as fascinated as ever by the origins of people. And it would be in keeping with her idea that one of their ancestors could have come from the Middle East, because the word gypsy was derived from the word Egyptian and had been given to the groups of wanderers when they had first turned up in England in the sixteenth century.

On the other hand, she argued with herself, the black hair and dark eyes could have been inherited from another race which had lived in the area long before any other people had settled here; the ancient Picts, those mysterious people about whom so little is known.

Absorbed in her historical back-trackings, Sandy did not hear the conversation which was going on between Nan and Lymond, and she jumped a little when Lymond pushed back his chair from the table.

'I suppose you have a bed ready where Sandy can sleep?' he said to Nan, as he stood up.

'Yes, I have, in the nursery wing, next to the wee bairn.'

Lymond's eyebrows lifted and his mouth curved in a smile.

'And I suppose you're going to tell me you've put her in there because you knew she was coming here to mind the boy, even though Martha neglected to inform me of the invitation she had extended to her cousin to stay the summer with us,' he said drily.

Nan's eyes widened and she looked quickly at Sandy and then back to Lymond.

'No, I put her in there because I thought she would be only a young lassie herself and would want to be near her cousin.' She paused, looking troubled, then said anxiously, 'You'll not be sending her back to England straight away, Lymond? You'll not be refusing her hospitality just because Martha wasn't completely honest with you?'

'No, he isn't sending me back. When I realised what had happened I offered to go back tomorrow, after I've seen

26

Martha,' explained Sandy hurriedly. 'What time can I get a bus from Kirkton to Dumfries?'

There was a strained silence. Lymond stared down at her, and Sandy had a feeling that it was the first time he had really looked at her; he took so long about it, his dark gaze going over her fair-skinned, slightly flushed face as if he hoped to find an answer to some problem there.

'Forget about the bus to Dumfries,' he said suddenly, as if he had come to a decision. 'Now that you're here you might as well stay for a couple of weeks, if it will help Martha and the boy. But remember always that this is my house and that you're my guest here, because I have just invited you to stay.'

There was no softening of his clean-cut face as he spoke, but his voice was no longer cool and indifferent. It had the hard ring of authority in it.

'Thank you,' Sandy said faintly, and wondered whether she should stand up and make a curtsey to him.

He nodded, swung on his heel and went out of the room. Sandy glanced at Nan, her eyes wide and puzzled. The other woman laughed and poured more tea into her cup.

'There's no doubt that Lymond can be haughty when he wants,' she remarked. 'I've been wondering when he would assert his authority again. You see, since the arrival of your cousin, bringing the news of Crawford's death, he's been very quiet and withdrawn. He wouldn't have any of us think it, but the news upset him greatly, and in his own way he's been mourning the death of his brother. And then he's been suspicious of your cousin.'

'Oh, why is that?'

'He had no idea that Crawford had been married. She could have been an impostor.'

'But Martha wouldn't do anything like that. I know she wouldn't. She was really married to Crawford,' exclaimed Sandy.

'Lymond knows that too, now, because he has seen her

marriage lines, but he didn't believe her at first,' said Nan gently.

'Oh, how cynical of him,' said Sandy, bristling in loyal defence of her cousin.

'No, not cynical, dear, just cautious. Lymond knew his brother in the same way that you know your cousin, so he knew that there was the possibility that Crawford hadn't been married to Martha even if he had lived with her and been the father of her child.'

'Oh, I see. Yes, I understand now,' said Sandy, unable to prevent the colour rising in her cheeks but appreciative of Nan's delicate explanation of the situation.

'Did you ever meet Crawford?' asked Nan, who was obviously eager for information about occasions which had happened beyond the limits of her life at Duncreggan. 'Were you present when they were married?'

'No, I wasn't. They were married in Paris. Martha was there modelling for a fashion house. She met Crawford at a party one night, and they were married three days later.'

Nan nodded. 'Yes, that's what she told us. It was very romantic, don't you think?'

'I suppose it was,' said Sandy with a laugh. 'We didn't see her again until she came home this spring with Dermid. Crawford seemed to move about a lot.'

'Aye, he was ever a restless one, yet he was the last one to leave Duncreggan,' sighed Nan, and picking up her cup began to sip her tea.

Sandy stood up and began to collect the dirty dishes together. Although she felt tired she was determined to show she was willing to help in the house.

'There's no need for you to do that,' objected Nan mildly.

'But I'd like to. I don't want to be any more trouble than I can help while I'm here. I wish Martha had asked Mr Caldwell's permission to invite me for the summer. Having to provide for Martha and Dermid is enough without hav-

28

ing me imposing on him as well,' said Sandy independently as she carried the dishes to the sink. 'So I must show I'm willing to work for my keep.'

'Och, I hope Lymond didn't give you the idea he's down to his last pound,' Nan laughed.

'He did mention he had a lot of debts to pay off and that the roof leaks. And it does look as if he needs a new car,' replied Sandy matter-of-factly, as she turned on the hot water tap.

'Aye, that's true,' said Nan, coming to the sink with more dishes. 'And I'm not saying he hasn't had a hard time of it making ends meet over the last two years so that he could clear those debts of Gavin's. But it's nearly done now.'

'Mrs Currie . . .'

'Call me Nan, dear, everyone does.'

'Have you any idea why Martha didn't ask him if she could invite me?'

'Aye, I do. I think she's a wee bit afraid of him.'

'That's what my mother said, guessing from the letter Martha wrote to me. But why should she be afraid of him?'

'I think it's because he looks like his brother but doesn't behave like him, and that puzzles her. One is often a little afraid of puzzles or mysteries. Don't you agree?'

'Until they're solved,' replied Sandy seriously. 'What was Crawford like?'

'By nature he was everything that Lymond isn't. He was noisy, gregarious, reckless, proud, easily hurt and quick to take offence. He could be charming the heart out of you one minute and sulking the next. He was always Gavin's favourite and yet they quarrelled in the end, too.' Nan sighed again, then added, 'If only Crawford had let Gavin know about Dermid it would have made all the difference. It would have bridged the gulf which had widened between them over the years.'

Sandy longed to ask what the quarrel had been about,

but she could see that Nan was troubled by the memories which had already been stirred, so she continued with the washing up in silence.

When she had finished she would have dried the dishes, too, but Nan, who had been pottering about putting leftovers of food away in a big walk-in larder, had other ideas.

'No, you've done enough, dear,' she murmured. 'And I can see you're fairly dropping with weariness, so I'll show you to your room.'

'But I'd like to see Martha first,' protested Sandy.

'In the morning,' said Nan placidly yet firmly. 'Everything will be better then. The sun will be shining on the sands, turning them to silver, the birds will be singing and all will be right. I'll tell Martha you've come when she returns. Come along, now.'

Sandy gave in and followed her up the stairs to the second floor. The nursery wing was at the end of a long landing and consisted of three rooms, a playroom and two bedrooms.

'The laddie is in there,' whispered Nan, pointing to a slightly open door beyond which a light flickered. 'He was frightened of the dark and the creaks in the house when he first came, so I gave him a night-light. You're in this room, next to him. It's small, but there's a view of the old castle and the Firth beyond it from the window. Is there anything else you'd like to know before I leave you?'

'I'd like the answers to two questions, please,' said Sandy. 'You see, if I don't ask them they'll bother me all night and keep me awake.'

'I understand. Ask away, then.'

'Firstly, who is Johnnie?'

'Och now, that's easy. He's my son, my one and only child. He's a fine braw lad, a wee bit younger than yourself, I'd say, just twenty-one. He's lived here all his life. I came to keep house just after Johnnie was born. I had nothing, you see, for Johnnie's father was killed when a tractor ran over him on the farm which we used to rent from Gavin. Johnnie is working for Lymond for the summer. Like yourself he's a student. He has friends down at the yacht club and he took Martha with him tonight to give her a wee outing. Now what's your other question?'

'What does Mr Caldwell do to make ends meet?'

'He looks after the estate, dear. Not that there is as much of it as there used to be. Lymond sold the farms which used to be rented to the farmers who worked them. And then he sold the land which lies on the other side of the brae to Gordon Carson the builder. He needed the money to pay some of the debts and to make the estate productive again.'

'But what does he do with the land—to make money, I mean?' persisted Sandy. She was still worried about Martha and herself imposing upon the hospitality of Lymond, who might not be able to afford non-paying unproductive guests in his house.

'He has a good herd of beef cattle, some dairy cattle, some sheep, a few chickens, and he's just started keeping pigs,' replied Nan, with her vague sweet smile.

'Oh, he's a farmer,' exclaimed Sandy.

'Aye, I suppose that's what you'd be calling him now, although Gavin would have preferred him to have gone into the army like himself. But Lymond was always keen on growing things and working with animals. It was disagreement over how the estate should be looked after which caused trouble between him and Gavin, and that was why he went away. He's lived and worked on farms in many different countries, mostly in the Commonwealth. Is that all you want to know, dear?'

'Yes, thank you. It explains why there was a pig in the back of the car,' said Sandy, who was glad that at least one small mystery was solved satisfactorily.

'Aye, it does. I'll leave you now. Goodnight, and sleep well.'

31

Although the bed was hard and narrow, the coarse white sheets were clean and smelt wholesomely of the fresh clear air in which they had been dried. Sandy fell asleep at once and slept all night. But towards morning she dreamed that she was locked up in the dungeon of a castle and, in the way of dreams, she was able to watch the approach of her rescuer even though she was still in the dungeon. He came galloping up on a black horse and he wore the armour of a medieval knight. A plume of black feathers waved in his helmet and when he strode into the dungeon, his sword in his hand, he lifted his visor and she found herself looking into the cool black eyes of Lymond Caldwell.

CHAPTER TWO

THAT first morning at Duncreggan, Sandy awoke suddenly out of her vivid dream to find herself alone in the small bedroom. Sunlight streamed in through a gap left by the shabby green velvet curtains which didn't quite cover the single sash window. Through the opening of the window came the sound of bird song.

Other noises penetrated too—a regular clanging sound like metal being banged against metal. It stopped and she heard men's voices calling to each other. Then there was the roar of an engine starting up, the clash of gears being changed and the rumble she associated with the movement of a heavy vehicle.

Springing out of bed, Sandy ran to the window, pushed back the curtains and looked out. The room was at the back of the house and overlooked a yard around which clustered white-painted farm buildings. A lorry loaded with milk churns was just grinding out of the yard. A young man dressed in jeans, shirt, sleeveless V-necked pullover

32

and rubber boots was standing in the yard watching the lorry depart. When it had gone he put his fingers to his mouth, whistled shrilly, and a black and white dog appeared. He spoke to it, and together man and dog went into one of the buildings. In a few seconds black and white cows came out, moving with their slow majestic swaying walk.

Sandy looked away from the yard. Beyond the curve of a green field the bulk of a tower rose, its grey stone shimmering softly in the early sunlight. It stood on a green knoll of land, and behind it the blue water of the Firth twinkled with reflected light. The tower was square, with narrow slitted windows, and the sight of it, an expression of the power and strength which had once belonged to the Caldwell family, gave Sandy the old familiar leap of excitement which any place of historical significance brought to her.

A shrill whistle made her look down at the yard. The young man had come out of the barn and was looking up at her. His face was split by a grin. Having caught her attention he waved cheerily. She waved too, and ducked back into the room.

She had just finished dressing when there was a knock at the door. She opened it and found Nan standing there holding a cup and saucer. Nan was wearing an old woollen dressing gown and her hair hung in a plait over one shoulder. Clutching her gown was two-year-old Dermid, and as Sandy noticed him he hid his chubby face behind Nan.

'I've brought you a cup of tea,' said Nan. 'Did you sleep well?'

'Fine, thanks,' replied Sandy, taking the tea. 'And thanks for bringing the tea. But don't do it every morning. I'm quite good at getting up early and need no persuasion. Hello, Dermid. Remember me?'

The little boy peeped out at her and nodded his head silently. His straight black hair was obviously inherited from his Caldwell father, but his eyes were like Martha's, wide and golden, almost catlike in their unblinking stare.

'He's needing his breakfast, so I'll take him down to the kitchen,' said Nan. 'Martha is still asleep, and no wonder. She and Johnnie didn't get back until after midnight.'

'Yet he's up early,' said Sandy, after sipping some of her tea.

'Aye, kicked out of bed by Lymond to see to the cows. It's his job for the summer, seeing that they're brought in to be milked and that the milk is loaded on to the lorry every morning,' said Nan. 'Would you be liking some porridge and cream for your breakfast, followed by bacon and eggs?'

'That sounds an awful lot to eat,' Sandy laughed.

'I'll be cooking it for Johnnie, so you may as well have it too. Lymond has had his breakfast and is away to Kirkcudbright for most of the day, at a meeting,' replied Nan. She fondled Dermid's dark head. 'Come along now, wean,' she said to him. 'We'll see what we can find for you to eat.'

When Sandy arrived in the kitchen, the young man who had whistled at her from the farmyard was already sitting at the table and was spooning up porridge from a bowl. Dermid was sitting in an old-fashioned wooden high chair with a bib tied round his neck and was doing his best to feed himself with porridge.

'Sit down, Sandy,' said Nan, putting a bowl of porridge at the place which was set opposite the young man. 'This is Johnnie. Sandy is Martha's cousin, lad.'

'Hello,' said the young man with a grin. His hair was black too and hung straight to his shirt collar at the back while it was cut in a fringe above his eyebrows. His features were broad, showing none of the fine chiselling noticeable in the faces of Nan and Lymond. 'Welcome to Duncreggan. Looks as if you've brought some fine weather with you. It's about time too. Martha was telling me last

34

night that you've just graduated in history. What are you going to do? Teach?'

'No, at least not yet.' He was easy to get on with, relaxed and open. Nothing dour or secretive about him. 'I'm going on to try for a second degree. What are you doing?'

'Forestry. I've another year before I get my degree. Then I'd like to move around a bit, work in other countries in the same way that Lymond did, to get experience. If you're interested in history you're going to like this place,' he chatted affably. 'You can hardly walk about without falling over some old ruin.'

'I noticed the castle this morning. I'd say it was built in the fourteenth century,' said Sandy. 'Have you any idea how long the Caldwells have held the land here?'

'No use asking *me* a question like that. My period is strictly mid-twentieth century,' he answered with a laugh. 'Do you know when the first Caldwell came here, Mother?' he asked as Nan removed his porridge bowl and set a plate of bacon and eggs in front of him.

'Gavin once told me that the family was descended from a Norman knight, a certain Sir Guy who came to help King David the First in his reforms in Scotland.'

'That would be earlier, in the twelfth century,' said Sandy, feeling pleased that her theory of the previous day had been proved right.

'Aye, that's so,' said Nan. 'And Gavin used to say there had been more than one building on this site. He believed there'd been an even earlier settlement, and he was forever digging in the ground.'

'Excavating, you mean?' exclaimed Sandy excitedly.

'Aye, or trying his hand at it. He said he was looking for pieces of jewellery or bits of pottery. He said they would help to tell him the exact period of that early settlement. He was writing the history of Duncreggan, you see.'

'What happened to his manuscript? Was it published?' demanded Sandy.

'Och, no. He died before it was finished. It's there in the library, pages and pages of writing,' sighed Nan.

'Do you think I could read it?' asked Sandy, looking at Johnnie because Nan had moved away to the cooker again. He shrugged his big shoulders.

'You'd have to ask the boss, none other than the present Knight of Duncreggan. The library must be in a terrible mess. The old man would never let any of us go in there,' he replied. 'But I hope history isn't your only interest. Have you ever done any sailing?'

'Yes. My brother and I own a dinghy. We take it to the south coast at the weekends to sail it.'

'Then perhaps you'd like to go out here some time. A friend of mine, Ron Carson, has just bought a twenty-five-foot sloop and is hoping to race it. How about coming out with us on Sunday?'

'I'd like to, but I'm not sure yet what Martha will want me to do. I've really come to help her by looking after Dermid occasionally, and not for a holiday.'

His brown eyes opened wide with surprise as if, like Lymond, he could not understand why Martha needed any help.

'She's quite a woman, isn't she?' he remarked. 'She has no time for all that business about Women's Lib. She likes to be admired for what she has in the way of physical attributes, but she makes darn sure it's known she isn't easy to get. How long are you staying?'

'I'm not sure. It depends on . . . on . . .' Sandy found suddenly she wasn't sure what she should call Lymond Caldwell. If he were truly a knight, perhaps she should call him Sir Lymond.

'On the boss,' Johnnie finished for her, his grin widening.

'Is he really a knight?' she asked.

'Better than that, the title is hereditary, it's really a baronetcy,' explained Nan, as she brought a plate of bacon and egg to Sandy. 'More tea, Johnnie?'

'No, thanks. I'd better get to work. One of the tractors is giving trouble and I promised Lymond I'd have a look at it.'

Sandy ate her breakfast and helped Dermid to finish his. She took the dirty dishes to the sink and would have washed up, but Nan would not let her.

'Och, no. You leave the laddie with me and take this tray up to Martha. It'll give her a wee surprise, and the two of you can have a blether. You'll find her in the room opposite the nursery.'

By daylight the hallway appeared shabbier than ever. As she went slowly up the uncarpeted stairs and along the passage Sandy gazed at the big gilt-framed pictures on the walls. Most of them depicted dark-browed, dark-eyed men, each one wearing the military uniform of an army officer of his period, all of whom, so the plaques below each picture stated, had been at one time or another Knights of Duncreggan.

She entered Martha's room carefully, found her way to the bedside table and placed the tray on it. Then she went to draw back heavy brocade curtains from two long windows which overlooked the driveway.

On either side of the drive the green pastures, where black-and-white cows grazed contentedly, rolled down to the grey winding ribbon of the main road. Beyond, the land rose more steeply. Rough grass and gorse bushes covered it, and shaggy wind-bent Scots pines clustered around heaps of grey rock. Above, the sky was a pale washed-out blue.

'Sandy, oh, Sandy, you've come! I'm so glad to see you.'

Martha had awakened and was sitting up in a big old-fashioned bed with brass railings at either end. A pale green nightdress was slipping off one of her smoothly-curved white shoulders and her red-gold hair was waving riotously around her perfect oval face. She held out her arms and Sandy went across to sit on the edge of the bed and hug her.

'I've brought your breakfast. You'd better eat it before it goes cold,' Sandy said when the affectionate embrace was over. Lifting the tray, she placed it in front of Martha.

'Thanks. You are a love,' replied Martha.

'It was Nan's idea.'

'Is Dermid with her?'

'Yes, she said she'd keep an eye on him.'

'Good. Then you and I can have a heart-to-heart chat. It's going to be lovely having you here. You've no idea how much I've longed to have someone of my own to talk to. Nan is very kind, but she's a little strange, and of course she won't hear of any criticism of this place or of the Caldwells.' Martha paused to munch some toast, then said, 'What do you think of the house, Sandy? Isn't it a scream? All the old-fashioned furnishings, the mildew and dry rot and the dim lighting? Perfectly Gothic, I thought, the day I arrived, and it comes complete with arrogant overlord.'

'You mean Sir Lymond?' asked Sandy.

'Yes, I mean him. But don't call him Sir to his face, Sandy. Aloof and arrogant he may be, but he detests formality. In fact to my way of thinking he could do with being a little more formal, but I suppose he got used to being casual about such things while he was living in Canada and the other countries where he's been. How did you get on with him on the drive from Dumfries?'

'Not very well. Martha, you should have asked him before you invited me to come and stay. It was most embarrassing when I realised he had no idea you'd invited me to come for the summer.'

Martha looked up, her eyes wide and catlike.

'How did you find out I hadn't asked him?' she inquired.

'He seemed cool and stand-offish, as if he hadn't wanted to meet me and didn't want me here, so I asked him out-

38

right if it was all right for me to stay for the rest of the summer.'

'Oh, Sandy, how could you let me down like that?'

'Let you down? I didn't let you down. How was I to know you hadn't asked him? Martha, why didn't you? It was only good manners to do so.'.

'I didn't ask him because I was afraid he would refuse, so I just asked you to come, thinking that once you were here he would agree to let you stay. That's what happened when I came. He said perhaps I'd like to stay for a while. I agreed and I'm still here. And I'm going to stay here until I get what I want.'

Silenced by her cousin's vehement statement of policy, Sandy watched while Martha disposed daintily of the last morsel of egg, wiped her fingers on the white linen table napkin Nan had provided and then finished sipping her tea. Martha, she thought, was one of those people who are born to be spoilt, who expect breakfast in bed and to be waited on by other people, and who assume they will always get what they want, and usually do.

'Don't you think it's a little like sponging on your brother-in-law to stay here longer than he expected when he invited you?' she said quietly.

'Take the tray, there's a love,' ordered Martha smoothly. 'And bring my hairbrush from the dressing table. I may as well be doing something useful while we're talking. Oh, and the hand mirror too, Sandy darling. You can hold it for me while I brush.'

Sandy did as she was asked, smiling a little to herself. Evidently she was to be milady's maid as well as nanny while she was at Duncreggan.

'You didn't answer my question,' she persisted, as she sat holding the mirror, and Martha flashed her an irritated glance.

'No, I don't think I'm sponging. After all, Crawford belonged here as much as Lymond does, and, as Crawford's widow, I think I have every right to be here, and Dermid has even more right.' She lowered the brush and reached out a hand to touch Sandy's arm. 'Don't look so worried. It'll be all right for you to stay, honestly it will. Once Lymond sees how good you are with Dermid he won't mind you being here.'

'It's not that I'm worried about. He's already invited me to stay for two weeks.'

'Has he? Then what's all the fuss about?'

'This feeling I have, of imposing upon him. Martha, couldn't you come back to Hampshire with me, today? You could get a job. It would be better than sponging.'

'Get a job? Oh, come off it, Sandy. I can do only one thing—modelling—and that would mean dieting first to get into shape, and even then I couldn't be sure of employment. And who would look after Dermid?'

'I'm sure Mother would. She wanted you to stay with her and Dad.'

'No, it wouldn't do. I'm staying here,' asserted Martha. 'You see, I've discovered I am *someone* here, and you know me, I like to be liked. The Caldwells, for all their dubious reputation in the past and their present poor financial state, are well known in this district and the name still carries some weight with it. Sir Gavin, although he was a bit eccentric, was a war hero, and Lymond has just been elected as a county councillor.'

'I'd no idea that social standing was so important to you', scoffed Sandy.

'It wasn't once, but now I've felt what it's like to have some. People want to know me here because I'm Crawford Caldwell's widow, Sir Gavin's daughter-in-law and Sir Lymond's sister-in-law, so I'm staying. And if I can get Lymond to accept Dermid and give him what should have been Crawford's share of the estate, I'll be happy.'

'But there was no money, Martha, only land,' exclaimed

Sandy, a little taken back by this new aspect of her cousin.

'How do you know?'

'He told me on the drive from Dumfries.'

'My my, he did talk to you a lot, didn't he?' jibed Martha. 'I know nothing was willed to Crawford, but that doesn't mean nothing can be done for his son. All I want for Dermid is the same education at a good school that Crawford had, even if Lymond has to pay for it out of his own pocket. I think he owes that to the only son of his twin brother. After all, Dermid is the only heir to this place so far.'

'I suppose so,' muttered Sandy, frowning as she picked at a loose thread in the bedcover. 'But I don't see where I come into your plan. How can I help?'

'You can make Dermid behave,' sighed Martha, leaning back against the pillows. 'Honestly, Sandy, he's been abominable since we came here, and he always behaves badly in front of Lymond. I noticed when we were with you in Hampshire he did everything you said, and that you could get him to behave himself in front of other people. I'd be glad if you could get it into his head somehow that Lymond is the person he has to impress and not Bob Stott or Will Brodie.'

'Who are they?'

'Two of the workers on the estate. And he just adores Johnnie, which is no help at all.'

'I suppose it's because they take time to talk to him and show him things,' mused Sandy. 'Doesn't Lymond?'

'I think he would, only Dermid always runs away when he sees him, or starts to scream blue murder.' Martha raised her sweeping eyelashes and gave Sandy a long, considering look. 'You seem to have got off to a good start with the Knight of Duncreggan, so you might have a go at softening him up.'

'Soften him up? How?' exclaimed Sandy.

'Oh, Sandy, you are an innocent! By using your feminine

41

wiles, silly. He's already invited you to stay, so you're off to a head start, I'd say.'

'I couldn't and wouldn't do such a thing,' retorted Sandy with a little shudder. 'I'm not the type. Have *you* tried softening him up, as you call it? You must be far more experienced at that sort of thing than I am.'

Martha smiled, that secretive, taunting little smile which must have driven some men crazy, thought Sandy irritably.

'I've tried and I'm still trying, love. But he's hard, not at all like Crawford. It's difficult to find a chink in his armour. I just thought that, being a little different from the usual run of women, you might find that chink. From all accounts he's not averse to feminine charms and had quite a reputation with the girls before he went abroad. You know, Sandy love, you'd be very attractive if only you'd get out of those awful pants.'

'I find them very comfortable and economical,' replied Sandy sharply, putting down the mirror and getting to her feet as she found the conversation becoming more and more annoying. She picked up the tray and looked down at her cousin. 'It's time you got up. You'll get fat if you stay in bed too long.'

Martha made a face at her and stretched her arms above her head.

'All right, little cousin, I can take a hint. But one day, Sandy, I'm warning you, you'll want some man to see you as a woman and not just as another person. It happens to us all sooner or later. Then you'll be in trouble . . .'

'What shall I do with Dermid this morning?' asked Sandy, ignoring the jibe as she opened the door.

'Take him to the beach. He loves playing there. I'll see you later.'

Dermid was quite happy to show Sandy the way to the beach and trotted along the road serenely, one small warm hand pushed into hers, the other grasping his bucket and spade.

To Sandy's pleased surprise, after fifteen minutes' walk the road dipped down to a horseshoe bay of twinkling water edged by clean firm sand which was backed by clusters of jagged sandstone rocks. The road ran between the beach and a crescent of houses, some of them renovated fishermen's cottages and others bigger and more modern in design. All were painted white and glistened in the hazy sunlight.

There were already children and young people playing on the beach, and Dermid soon found the friends he had made on a previous visit. They were a small girl about his own age with swinging silky hair and deep blue eyes who was called Lorna, and her brother Euan, an excitable scamp of about three and a half, who had rusty red hair and freckles. They were supervised by a middle-aged nanny who sat on one of the seats set about on the grass between the road and the sands, and who made no attempt to play with them or to speak to Sandy.

The morning passed quickly as Sandy played ball, made sandpies, dug channels and paddled in the cool placid water. The other children were called to go for their dinner, and, after promising to see them again, Sandy took Dermid back to Duncreggan. There she found that Martha had taken advantage of the opportunity to accompany Johnnie who had had to go into Kirkton: she would visit the hairdresser and would not be back until three o'clock.

After dinner Sandy took Dermid up to his room for his afternoon nap, and then went to her own room to write to her parents to tell them she had arrived safely and to give them news of Martha and Dermid. When it was written and the envelope addressed, she put it in her pants pocket, intending to post it when she went down to the beach that afternoon.

Going over to the window, she looked out at the formidable bulk of the castle. Its grey stone shimmered in the sunlight and behind it the shining waters of the Firth slid silently by. She recalled her dream of the previous night. Was there a dungeon in the cellar of the castle? She glanced at her watch. Dermid would sleep for another half-hour at least. That was enough time for her to take a closer look at the castle and perhaps even find the places where Gavin Caldwell had once tried his hand at excavating.

Within minutes she was out of the house and walking along a winding path edged by two drystone walls over which honeysuckle tumbled in profusion. The sweet smell of the flowers, the soft stillness of the warm air, the distant sound of waves falling on an unseen shore, all combined to create an atmosphere of another, older world, so that she felt as if, in walking along the path, she was stepping into the past.

The feeling was increased when the path ended suddenly, giving way to a grass-covered slope which dipped down into a hollow, then rose steeply to form the mound on which the castle was built. The hollow was the filled-in moat, Sandy decided as she ran down into it and climbed up the other side. Above her the walls of the tower reared up, rough and silvery grey, flat and sheer, up to the broken battlements, jagged pieces of stone, stark against the moving blue of the sky.

Walking round a corner of the tower, she found that double doors had been set into the wall that faced east, and that a rough roadway led from them over a narrow wooden bridge which spanned the hollow left by the moat; then wound away through a small wood to the main road.

One of the double doors was slightly open, so she approached it and peeped round the edge. Immediately her impression that she had stepped back to the Middle Ages was destroyed, for the square room seemed full of old cars.

There was an elegant electric-blue Rolls-Royce, built, she guessed, round about 1910. Next to it was a green Bentley sports car about 1930 vintage with a long bonnet, held down by a strap, and black leather seats. Beside these two aristocratic giants, an original Austin Seven looked tiny and just a little bit cheeky.

Realising that they were the cars which had belonged to Crawford, Sandy looked round the room. There was a large stone fireplace against one wall and she decided, as she recalled all that she knew about medieval castles, that the room must have once been the kitchen.

In one corner she found a circular staircase built into the wall. She mounted the spiralling steps, carefully noting how worn the stone was in the middle of each one where so many feet had trodden.

The staircase brought her out into a big empty room with a high raftered roof. Sunlight shafted in through the narrow, glassless windows. Watching carefully where she stepped, in case any of the floorboards might be rotten, she went to the nearest window and looked down on to the shining waters of the Firth. The haze of the morning had lifted, and she could see right across to the distant hills of England.

Looking back into the room, she decided it must have been the great hall. Here the family must have gathered for meals, and it wasn't difficult for her to imagine a huge table set with mugs and platters around which ladies wearing long gowns and high wimpled headgear sat with men who wore leather jerkins and hose. She could even imagine the hunting dogs sprawling under the table, waiting for bones.

Returning to the staircase, she mounted carefully to the next floor and found herself out in the open air; the roof of the castle had long since gone and all that was left of the two rooms which she suspected had been there were two fireplaces on the north wall.

She glanced at her watch. It was time to make her way back to the house, so she returned to the ground floor. She hadn't found the dungeon, but there would be other days when she could come exploring.

Edging round the three cars, she made for the doors, and it wasn't until she reached out a hand to open one that she became aware that something was different. Had she shut the door which had been open behind her? She couldn't really remember. She had been too surprised by the sight of the cars to notice.

She tried the door. It didn't move, and with a tingle of shock she realised it was locked. Someone must have come and locked it while she had been upstairs.

If she didn't act quickly she might be locked in there for the rest of the day, possibly all night. She hurried up the staircase to the next floor. Crossing to the north wall, she peered through a window. Yes, someone was walking away up the other side of the hollow. If she called she might be able to attract attention. Leaning over the stone still, she cupped her hands round her mouth and yelled as loudly as she could.

'Hey, you, come back here! You've locked me in.'

The striding figure stopped, half-turned and looked back. Then, evidently deciding that he had imagined her shout, he turned away to stride on towards the house. Sandy yelled again and followed her yell with a piercing whistle. The figure halted again and this time turned right round and began to walk down into the hollow of the moat.

Within a few seconds Sandy was able to see who he was, none other than Caldwell of Duncreggan himself, and soon he was standing on the grass below her. Hands on his hips, his head tipped back, he looked up at her, and although she was several feet above him she felt the shock of his black glance, and for a moment felt as if she were back in her dream of the previous night.

'What are you doing up there?' he asked.

Slanting sunlight from the west gave his face a bronze tint which seemed to emphasise the straight lines of brow and nose and the tough angle of the jawbone. He was dressed in a suit of fine grey tweed and a conventional

46

shirt and tie, and she remembered he had been to a meeting.

'Admiring the view. What else?' she retorted sweetly, and felt a strange jolt of pleasure when he smiled in appreciation of her mockery. The smile robbed his face of austerity and hinted at a sense of humour which was not always on show. 'Please will you unlock the door so I can get out?' she pleaded.

He stared at her as if giving her request serious consideration before granting it.

'Perhaps I should keep you locked up,' he suggested and as she moved sharply in protest he added quickly, 'Oh, I'd feed you. I'd bring you pasties of meat, platters of fresh fish, bowls of fruit and flagons of wine from the table in the house. I'd bring them at nightfall when no one is about because I wouldn't want anyone to know I have a fair damsel locked up in my tower. We'd sit by candlelight and share the food and the wine, and afterwards . . .' He stopped speaking and looked down at the bunch of keys he had taken from his trouser pocket, then looked up again. 'I'll let you out,' he said coolly, and Sandy, who had been enchanted by the fantasy he had been weaving and which had included her, blinked as he moved out of her sight on his way to the doors.

Still feeling strange, as if under a spell cast by a magician, half expecting to see the skirt of a long gown swirling about her feet as she went down the spiral staircase, she was jolted back into reality by the sight of the old cars. The door was open and Lymond was standing by it waiting for her, his face taut and unsmiling, his eyes blank and empty as they met her wide puzzled gaze.

'It was foolish of you to come in here and go upstairs alone,' he said curtly. 'The floor up there isn't safe. And then you could have been here all night if I hadn't heard you call from the window.'

'How was I to know you'd come and lock the door? It

47

was open when I came, so I supposed it was always left open,' she retorted. No wonder Martha found him puzzling. One minute he was weaving fantasies, the next he was giving you a cold set-down.

'Johnnie must have left it open when he came to get some tools to work on the tractor. We use this ground floor as a storage place for pieces of machinery and engine parts. I keep it locked because the cars have some antique value,' he replied.

'They were Crawford's,' she said. 'Are you going to let Dermid have them?'

He gave her a narrowed suspicious glance.

'Did you come here this afternoon to see them?' he queried, ignoring her question.

'No, I'd no idea they were here. I wanted to see the castle to find out if there's a dungeon in it, but I couldn't find a way down to the cellar.'

'The way is over there, in the corner by a trap-door in the floor. Would you like to see it now?' he inquired politely.

'Not now, thank you. There isn't time. Dermid might be awake and wondering where I am.' She slipped past him through the door, out into the warmth of the August sunlight. He followed her, locked the door, and together they went down into the hollow of the moat and up the other side.

'Why are you so interested in the castle's dungeon?' he asked.

'I dreamed last night that I was locked in it,' she replied. 'But I'm interested in the castle as a whole. Nan told me this morning that your father was writing a history of Duncreggan from the very earliest times.'

'Are you interested in history?' he asked.

'Yes, I've just taken my B.A. in it at Dulchester University. I specialised, actually, in what is known as prehistory, that's archaeology, and I've helped at the excavations of various sites in the south of England.'

They were sauntering along the path now. The buzzing of bees seeking nectar from the honeysuckle seemed to emphasise the somnolence of the warm afternoon.

'No one would suspect you share the same blood as Martha,' Lymond observed suddenly, and Sandy gave him a surprised sidelong glance.

'No, I don't suppose they would,' she agreed. 'You see, we both take after our mothers in appearance. Martha's father was my mother's brother. But Martha's beauty is unique in our family.'

'I wasn't thinking of physical likenesses. They're not really very important. I was thinking of attitudes and interests,' he replied.

'Well, from what I've heard you and your brother were very different, even though you looked alike, so there's much more likelihood of cousins being different,' she offered.

'And what have you heard in the short time you've been here?' he queried softly, and she realised that she had unwittingly stepped on to dangerous ground. As if by mutual consent they both stopped walking and turned to face each other. Enclosed as the path was at this point by stone walls and shaggy hedges, it was like being in a flower-scented arbour, cut off from the outside world.

'I've heard that he was everything that you're not,' she said, refusing to be intimidated by hard black gaze.

'Your cousin's opinion, perhaps?' he scoffed. 'I suspect he gave in to her all the time, let her have her own way. He was always a sucker for female blandishments.'

'And you are not?' she challenged.

'I prefer to be the one who calls the tune in any relationship.'

'I know that Martha seems a little flighty and frivolous

to you, but I'm sure she loved your brother truly,' she said earnestly. 'And his child,' she added, remembering the task that had brought her to Duncreggan.

His dark eyebrows lifted. A muscle twitched at one corner of his mouth. A small flame seemed to dance in the depths of his dark eyes, and, seeing it, Sandy braced herself for an ironic remark.

'You believe that such an emotion exists, then, in spite of all your reading of history?' he scoffed.

'Yes, I do,' she replied staunchly. 'It's because of my reading of history that I do. Don't you believe it exists?'

'I think it's a word which women often use to disguise their own self-interest,' he replied coolly.

'Oh, how horrid and cynical you are!' she blurted, forgetting all about having to make an impression on him and soften him up. 'I suppose you believe that Martha was thinking only of herself when she married your brother. That she was putting herself first when she came here.'

He folded his arms across his chest and looked down at her as if she were a child in need of guidance.

'Wasn't she?' he asked softly, tauntingly.

'No, she wasn't. She came here because your brother asked her to come, for Dermid's sake . . .'

'And that's why she's outstaying her welcome?' he suggested, and for a moment she hesitated. Then, realising he had interrupted her deliberately to put her off balance, she gathered herself together and launched another attack.

'What else can she do? She's waiting for you to do something for Dermid. Surely it isn't too much for her to ask you to do the right thing for your brother's child?'

'So that's it.' The twist at the corner of his mouth wasn't pleasant. 'You know, it's a pity Martha can't speak her own mind and has to use you as a go-between. What exactly is it that she wants for Dermid?'

'I . . . I . . . really think you should discuss it with her,' gasped Sandy, realising that Martha had put her in another embarrassing situation. 'Hasn't she ever approached you about it?'

He shook his head.

'Not directly. Whenever I've attempted to talk about the future I'm treated to floods of tears.' He lifted his shoulders in a shrug. 'I'm afraid I've no time for that sort of scene.'

No chink in his armour, Martha had said, having tried, without success, her usual tactic of being a soft helpless female. But how did one get through to the living, feeling man beneath the armour?—presuming that there was one there and not just a hollow emptiness?

The sound of voices drew the attention of both of them. Dermid appeared round a bend in the path and behind him came Martha, her red-gold hair catching fire from the sunlight and creating a halo round her head, giving an impression of saintliness which was borne out by the creamy oval of her straight-nosed face; until perhaps one noticed the provocative sensual curve of her full red lips.

'Oh, there you are, Sandy. Dermid was looking for you when I got back from Kirkton,' she said. Then she glanced sideways at Lymond from under fluttering, darkened eyelashes. 'Hello, Lymond,' she said softly. 'It's nice of you to show my little cousin around the estate.'

At this obvious attempt to vamp Lymond, Sandy's heart sank. Couldn't Martha see that she was only irritating him and laying herself open to some of his more caustic remarks? As she watched, Lymond stared insolently at Martha, his glance, suddenly bold, flickering over her prettily curved figure, which was shown to advantage in an attractive summer dress made from some soft clinging green and white material.

Then she was surprised as he turned and looked at herself, closed one of his eyes in a conspiratorial wink and said,

'But I haven't been showing your cousin round the estate. I've been rescuing a fair damsel from the castle. Will you excuse me, please. I have work to do.'

He walked away from them in the direction of the house and Martha stared after him, her mouth slightly open.

'Well, really!' she exclaimed. 'Isn't he the strangest person? Whatever did he mean? Do you know, Sandy?'

Sandy found she was having difficulty in suppressing the laughter which had bubbled up unexpectedly inside, so was unable to reply before Dermid piped up,

'What's a fair damsel, Sandy? Will I find one in the castle like Uncle Lymond did?'

'I don't think so,' she answered, her voice shaking a little. 'You see, fair damsels are usually only met "in forests wide by knights of Logres or of Lyones",' she added, recalling an appropriate line from *Paradise Lost*.

'What's a knight?' persisted Dermid.

'A man on a horse who goes about doing good deeds and rescuing fair damsels from dragons and imprisonment.'

'Uncle Lymond doesn't ride a horse,' corrected Dermid, who was a stickler for detail.

'That was in the old days. Now they drive cars, or fly aeroplanes or . . .'

'Really, Sandy, you're as bad as Lymond with his fair damsels! Whoever heard of a knight in armour driving a fast car or flying an aeroplane?' said Martha impatiently as they walked along the path.

'Isn't that how you saw Crawford when you first met him?' challenged Sandy, and Martha gave her a rather puzzled glance.

'Johnnie is a knight,' said Dermid, who was obviously enraptured by the idea. 'A knight on a motor-bike.' And at once he set off at full speed down the driveway to which they had come, imitating the throaty growl of a motor-bike's engine.

'Oh, stop him, Sandy, stop him! He might run out into the road and the cars come fast round the bend there,' cried Martha.

52

Sandy set off at once, sprinting after Dermid, thinking rather ruefully to herself that her little ploy to make Lymond seem attractive to his nephew hadn't worked out as she had hoped. Johnnie on his motor-bike was still more attractive to the child than the real knight was.

To her relief Dermid had shown sense and had stopped by the gateposts, and was standing there growling softly in imitation of an engine idling while he waited for her and Martha. Soon they were all walking along the road to the beach.

Once there Dermid found Lorna and Euan. Sandy would have joined in their play, but Martha said,

'They're all right. Let's sit down and talk.'

So they sat on one of the seats next to the one on which the Lindsay children's nanny sat. Once again the woman ignored their existence, much to Martha's amusement.

'She's a real old battleaxe, isn't she? Never speaks to anyone. They're such nice little children, too. Did you play with them this morning?'

'Yes. Do they live here?'

'Only in the summer. Their father is Bill Lindsay. He's an orthopaedic surgeon and he owns that big house, over there on the other side of the bay.'

Sandy identified the house, standing on its own on the long point of land that made one side of the bay. It was square and solid-looking and was painted white, in gleaming contrast to the dark trees which clustered about it. It seemed to have an extensive landscaped garden from which steps led down to the beach.

'Bill is vice-commodore of the yacht club this year,' Martha went on. 'I met him one evening when Johnnie took me down there. He and I have something in common. He's a widower—his wife died last year. I believe she had leukaemia.'

'Nan told me about him when I mentioned the children to her. She gave me the impression that the Lindsays and the Caldwells have never been exactly friendly. She said there was once a feud between the two families.'

'Nan and her feud,' scoffed Martha. 'What do you think of her? Isn't she odd? And so old-fashioned in the way she waits on Lymond and Johnnie as if they weren't capable of doing anything for themselves. One day she told me my fortune. She said I would marry again and that the man would be as different from Crawford as it's possible to be. I hope she's right, about the marriage part, I mean.'

'But it's only a few months since Crawford died. Surely you don't want to get married again so soon,' objected Sandy.

'I know. But I don't want to be a widow for the rest of my life,' said Martha, looking across to where the three children were playing on the edge of the sand, their figures silhouetted against the bright water which was shimmering with golden light from the sun. Then with a sudden change of subject she added, 'I wonder why Lymond keeps Nan on as housekeeper?'

'I suppose he could hardly turn her away, since she's a relative and has looked after the house for twenty years,' replied Sandy.

'And did more than keep house, if all the tales I've heard about her and Gavin Caldwell are true,' said Martha.

'What do you mean? More than kept house?' asked Sandy.

'There you go again!' laughed Martha. 'Honestly, Sandy, no one would ever think you're one of the present generation who are supposed to know everything and do everything and not be surprised by illicit or illegal relationships. From all accounts Major Sir Gavin Caldwell was a very attractive man and in her time Nan must have been good-looking in the dark Caldwell way. Can you really believe they could live together in the same house for all those years, both of them widowed, without something happening between them?'

'Yes, I can. Physical attraction isn't everything. I believe that men and women can live in the same house, can work in the same office or work-place without becoming either physically or emotionally involved with each other,' said Sandy.

Martha gave her a sidelong satirical glance.

'What can you possibly know about it? What experience have you had? You've only mixed with dedicated students of history and stuffy professors more interested in digging up the past than in what's going on around them. You've never lived in the same house as an attractive man.'

'I suppose Dad and brother Tom don't count,' retorted Sandy with an impish grin.

'You know they don't,' retorted Martha. 'Haven't you ever met a man you think you might like to marry and live with?'

Sandy thought of Derek Sloan, who was now far away excavating on an island in the Mediterranean Sea.

'Yes, in a way I have thought about it,' she admitted. 'I've met one.'

'Tell me about him,' ordered Martha, her face lighting up at the thought of sharing a confidence.

'There isn't much to tell,' laughed Sandy. 'As you guessed, he's one of those dedicated students. He and I have taken the same courses from our first year. We've talked about archaeology most of the time. We get excited about finding sherds of pottery when we've been excavating together. This summer I hoped to go to the Mediterranean with him on the same expedition, but I wasn't accepted and he was.'

'Oh, too bad, love. Why weren't you accepted?'

'They had enough people. I was among a long list of people who had to be turned down.'

'Do you miss him?'

Sandy glanced away at the glittering water of the bay, felt the sun's rays warm upon her face, heard the shouts of children at play and thought of the secrets of the past which lay hidden under the earth at Duncreggan.

'Not yet,' she answered honestly. 'Maybe I'll know by the end of the summer whether I've missed him.'

'Well, it doesn't sound like the real thing,' said Martha emphatically.

'How do you know when it's the real thing?' laughed Sandy. 'Do bells ring? Or do fireworks go off? What happened when you met Crawford?'

'I don't know. He didn't give me a chance to find out. We met at a party and before it had ended he was proposing to me. He was like that, crazy, impulsive. When he saw something he liked he had to have it.'

'And you were something he liked,' said Sandy dreamily.

'I must have been, mustn't I?' replied Martha lightly. 'But it's over now.'

'What do you mean, it's over?' said Sandy in a rather shocked whisper, a little horrified at the fickleness of her cousin's feelings in regard to people. 'Don't you miss him?'

'Not any more. You see, Sandy, I think Nan's prediction is going to come true. I think I've found someone else who is as different from Crawford as possible. And that's another reason why I must stay here, because he isn't impulsive like Crawford. He's slower, more cautious, and he'll have to be persuaded that it's the right thing for both of us to do, and persuasion takes time. It could take longer than the summer.'

Martha spoke slowly, seriously. Her curling red-gold hair slipped forward about her face as she leant forward and with a piece of driftwood she had picked up, she drew upon the firm damp sand. Sandy glanced down to see what she was drawing and felt a faint shiver of shock, for Martha was drawing a letter, and when she had finished, it stood out quite clearly. It was a bold capital 'L'.

It could stand for no other name but Lymond; Lymond who, according to Nan, was different in every way except looks from his twin brother. The question leapt into

Sandy's mind ready to be asked. She turned to Martha, but her cousin's attention had been attracted by the shrieks of Lorna and Euan. Both children were scampering across the sand towards a tall man with reddish hair who was coming across the beach from the direction of the big white house and who was accompanied by a tall elegantly-dressed woman.

'That's Bill Lindsay,' said Martha. 'The woman must be his sister Helen. She's a doctor and has just come back from South America where she's been working with the United Nations Organisation. I hope Bill sees us. I'd like you to meet him. I think you'll like him, and I'd like to meet his sister.'

Sandy watched the tall man lift Lorna in his arms as she ran up to him. He reached down a hand for Euan to take. A few yards away stood Dermid, his shoulders slumped, his face crumpling with unhappiness as he watched his friends being greeted by their father. Poor little Dermid, she thought. It was at times like this that he must miss his own father.

But Bill Lindsay had noticed Dermid too. He smiled and called out,

'Hello there, Dermid. Where's your mummy?'

At once Dermid's face lit up. He pointed with his little wooden spade at Martha and smiling happily fell into step beside Euan and Bill as they turned to approach the seat where Martha and Sandy sat. The tall woman came a few reluctant steps behind them.

Bill Lindsay's long-jawed face was plain, good-humoured and freckled like his son's.

'Hello, Martha. I see you're making the most of the sunshine while it's with us,' he said.

'It's lovely, isn't it?' said Martha brightly. 'I like to think it's been brought from the sunny south by my cousin Sandy here. She's come to stay at Duncreggan with me.'

As Sandy exchanged greetings with Bill the tall woman

glanced at Martha in surprise, then said rather super-ciliously,

'Duncreggan? Did you say you're staying at Duncreggan?'

'Yes. I'm Martha Caldwell. I'm staying with my brother-in-law Lymond,' answered Martha pleasantly.

'Martha is Crawford's widow,' put in Bill quietly.

A strange expression flashed across Helen Lindsay's face. She didn't acknowledge Martha, but, turning to her brother, said,

'We must go back to the house. Mother is waiting to see the children.'

She turned on her heel and went off across the sand, leaving behind her an awkward strained silence. She walked gracefully, her head well up and her shoulders straight. Her brown hair had the sheen of a chestnut in the sunlight.

Bill looked rather uncomfortable.

'Helen is feeling a little like a fish out of water, just now,' he murmured. 'You wouldn't think it to look at the place, but there have been quite a lot of changes here since she went away nearly five years ago. I hope you'll excuse me if I take the bairns back to the house. I'll be seeing you down at the yacht club, I expect, Martha?'

'I expect so,' said Martha.

Bill walked away with his two hopping and skipping children and Martha looked at Sandy, a rather wry smile curving her lips as she lifted her slim shoulders in a shrug.

'So that's what it's like to be snubbed.' She tried to speak lightly to cover up, but Sandy could see that tears were very near the surface of the big golden eyes. 'She didn't like me, did she? I wonder why?'

'Possibly because your name is Caldwell,' suggested Sandy. 'Perhaps she keeps up the feud.'

'Perhaps,' said Martha. She was very quiet on the way back to Duncreggan, so that Sandy guessed her apparently frivolous and superficial cousin had been hurt by Helen Lindsay's obvious snub.

58

THE warm sunny weather held for several days, and Sandy settled into the pleasant routine of taking Dermid to the beach every morning and afternoon. It was even warm enough to go swimming, and being a good swimmer herself she gave lessons to Dermid and his two little Lindsay playmates, splashing around in the shallow water of the pretty rock-rimmed bay.

Most days Martha was with them, but she never joined in their games, seeming content to talk to other people she had met on previous visits to the beach. Once or twice Bill Lindsay put in an appearance when he returned from his work early and joined her on the seat where she usually sat sunning herself, but his sister never appeared again and he never referred to her.

For Sandy the days were usually rounded off pleasantly with a trip to Creggan, a small village huddled close to the shore of a river estuary on the other side of the hill that rose at the back of Duncreggan House. She went with Johnnie, riding pillion on his motor-bike, going by way of the main road back in the direction of Kirkton, but turning off down a winding country lane which ended in the village.

Creggan delighted her. Once a small port and fishing village, it was now a centre for sailing and a holiday resort. All the original fishermen's cottages had been renovated and turned into holiday residences. They were strung out along the road bordering the estuary, the water of which reflected the blue sky as well as the green hills of the opposite shore.

When the tide was in the estuary was alive with small boats, their multi-coloured sails and pennants shimmering in sunlight and fluttering in light breezes. When the tide was out the river dwindled to a narrow channel winding like a blue snake between sleek mudbanks that changed colour from gold through bronze to dark brown according to the state of the sun.

It was in Creggan that Sandy met Ron Carson. A little older than herself, he was 'a thick-set young man with brown crinkly hair, blue eyes and a happy-go-lucky nature. He was an architect and a partner in his father's business. Often he took Sandy and Johnnie for a sail down the estuary in his small blue sloop, and on the one Sunday she had been at Duncreggan he had taken them for a delightful short cruise down the Firth and back, which had taken all day.

It was with a feeling or surprise, tinged with guilt, that Sandy awoke one morning and realised that she had been at Duncreggan for almost two weeks and had done nothing towards helping Martha to persuade Lymond to do something for Dermid. She had done nothing either to find out more about the history of Duncreggan. In fact all she had done was laze about and enjoy herself having a pleasant holiday at the expense of Martha's brother-in-law.

Guilt would not be stifled or ignored. She sprang out of bed. It was just after six o'clock. With a little luck she might catch Lymond in the kitchen before he started work on the estate.

For he was an elusive person, she had discovered. Although he always appeared at mealtimes he did not contribute much to the conversation, and after eating his meal silently and quickly would usually excuse himself and go off to his study to attend to the piles of paperwork associated with farming, or outside to supervise some project being carried out on the estate.

Certainly his aloofness was not making it easy for Martha to influence him on Dermid's behalf, thought Sandy, as she zipped herself into her jeans. Then she frowned as she remembered the capital 'L' Martha had once drawn in the sand.

Did Martha really intend to stay at Duncreggan until

Lymond responded to her attempts to attract him? Was she really interested in him as her next partner in marriage? There hadn't been many occasions when she had been able to observe Martha and Lymond together, but when she had she often found herself squirming with embarrassment at her cousin's rather obvious efforts to make up to him.

As for Lymond, who could tell what went on behind the unsmiling mask of his handsome face, or behind the blank dark eyes which so often surveyed each of them in turn at the meal table as if he were assessing each of them and drawing conclusions about them which he kept to himself?

Sandy gave her shining hair a quick brush, made a face at the reflection she saw in the mirror of a young woman who had a pink-cheeked face, broad-lipped generous mouth, retroussé nose and bright grey eyes set under arched finely etched eyebrows and who was dressed in a boy's shirt tucked into the waistband of faded blue jeans. Then she skipped out of the room and down the stairs just as the old grandfather clock in the dusty hallway chimed half-past six.

As she entered the kitchen she felt a flash of satisfaction. He was there, alone, eating porridge, his dark eyebrows slanting in a frown as he read something from a magazine which he had propped up against the teapot in front of him.

Sandy glanced round. No sign of Nan, and Johnnie would still be seeing to the cows, so she had Caldwell of Duncreggan to herself for a few minutes. Now was the time to strike.

'Good morning,' she greeted him brightly. She still hadn't decided how she should address him. 'It looks like another fine day.'

He looked up sharply; his eyes widened slightly, then narrowed.

'Good morning,' he replied abruptly, and went back to his magazine.

Not at all disturbed by his cool reception, Sandy went

over to the cooker and helped herself to porridge from the pan which was being kept warm there. As she turned back to the table it struck her suddenly that the kitchen, which was never very tidy, seemed more chaotic than usual. The table wasn't set with its usual bright cloth and she had to go and find herself a spoon and a cup and saucer. It was obvious that Nan was not up and about.

'Where's Nan?' she asked the uncommunicative man as she sat down opposite to him.

'She isn't feeling very well, so I told her to go back to bed. You'll have to see to your own meals today,' he replied curtly. Then he added coldly, 'It's time you and your cousin realised that this isn't a hotel or a boarding house.'

Surprise was followed by resentment at the unfairness of his unexpected attack, but Sandy was resolved to remain serene.

'I know it isn't,' she replied. 'And I do help Nan when I can. Could I be of help today while she stays in bed and rests?'

He gave her a narrowed searching glance as he leaned back in his chair.

'I doubt it,' he said slowly, and the lift of his eyebrows conveyed a scepticism about her abilities which flicked her pride.

'What do you think I am? Helpless?' she retorted spiritedly, and his mouth curved in a tantalising smile which gave him a sudden fleeting attraction.

'Oh, no, I wouldn't go so far as to say that,' he drawled. 'But I can hardly believe a degree in history has fitted you to take on the running of a house like this. Even Nan finds it a little too much at times, and she's been doing it for years. I don't want to hurt your feelings, but I think you'd find it beyond your abilities even for a day to prepare dinner and supper for all of us, clean and do the washing as well as do the jobs in the farmyard which Nan usually attends to.'

62

He was patronising and superior, an arrogant chauvinist who didn't bother to conceal his contempt for women like herself and Martha who hadn't been trained in the traditional role of housekeepers. And Sandy reacted accordingly.

'You know nothing of what I can do,' she retorted. 'I could all that I've seen Nan doing in a day, and more, and I'll prove it to you today, starting now!'

The black eyes returned her indignant glare. No expression flickered in them. Then they were hidden as he looked down at his empty teacup. The muscle at the corner of his mouth twitched slightly and for one moment she thought he was going to laugh at her, and wondered wildly what she would do if he did.

'You seem very determined to take over,' he drawled. 'Far be it from me to look a gift horse in the mouth. All right, I accept your challenge. Prove to me that you can do what Nan does every day.'

A little surprised by his sudden capitulation and slightly distrustful still of that curl at the corner of his mouth, Sandy retreated a few steps from her position.

'Only on one condition,' she parried.

The dark eyes lifted to regard her ironically. The firm mouth twisted unpleasantly.

'I might have known there would be a condition,' he said with a sigh of weary exasperation which made her want to hit him. 'What is it?'

'Please let me look at the history which your father was writing about Duncreggan,' she appealed. 'Nan says it's in the library. I'd like to have your permission to go in there and look for it.'

He stared blankly for a moment, obviously surprised.

'What a strange request,' he said. 'You can look at it if you wish, but I'm warning you the library is in one hell of a mess. My father wouldn't let anyone touch anything in it and I haven't bothered to put it to rights.'

'Have you any idea where he might have put the manuscripts?' she asked.

'Try the drawers in the desk,' he replied, and rose to his feet. Again his slightly mocking smile appeared as he glanced down at her. 'Is it a deal, then? In return for letting you rummage in the library will you cook dinner and supper, wash the dishes, tidy up, do the washing and so on?'

She nodded rather stiffly in agreement and he turned away to go outside without another word. Alone at the table Sandy looked round the kitchen, and for the first time she saw how antiquated the equipment was. There were none of those electrical gadgets she had used in her mother's kitchen. Now she realised what she had done. She had allowed herself to be tricked into doing a day's hard work. The overlord of Duncreggan had implied that she wasn't capable of doing it, and she had fallen right into his carefully baited trap. No wonder he had agreed so easily to her condition! And now he must be having a good laugh.

Furious with herself for having been out-manoeuvred, disliking Lymond Caldwell heartily for his superior mocking attitude towards her, she went upstairs to look in on Nan.

The woman was lying on her bed. Her face was white and drawn and there were dark circles under her eyes.

'It's the migraine,' she whispered. 'I get it periodically and have to stay in bed.'

'Well, you don't have anything to worry about today. I'm going to do the cooking and everything else, but it would help if you could tell me what meals you had planned for today,' said Sandy gently.

Nan told her what meat and vegetables she would find for dinner and what would be expected for supper or high tea; then went on to explain how the eggs had to be collected from the hen-houses and put in boxes ready to be transported the next day.

'It's good of you, lass, to help like this. I appreciate it, and I know Lymond will too.'

We'll see whether he does or not at the end of the day, thought Sandy rather grimly, as she went along to Martha's room to wake her cousin and tell her what had happened.

'Oh, Sandy, you silly goose!' exclaimed Martha crossly. She sat up in bed, her hair falling in wild ringlets round her saintly face and making her look like a Botticelli angel. 'Fancy falling for a trick like that! It would have to happen when I've been invited to play golf with the Irvines at the Kirkton club this afternoon. How could you let me down? It was for such occasions that I asked you to come and stay here, so that I could go off without having to worry about Dermid. You know, you don't have to do Nan's work. The men have managed before when she's been ill.'

'I suppose they have,' muttered Sandy, who was still smarting from Lymond's treatment of her. He must see her as a naïve girl, amusingly simple in her approach to life, to be taken advantage of and used. 'But I can't back out now. Lymond would never let me hear the end of it if I did. Anyway, I haven't much to do here, and helping for a day will make me feel better about staying.'

'Are you still feeling guilty about that?' asked Martha, giving her a curious glance.

'Yes, I am.' Sandy regarded Martha narrowly as an idea sprang into her mind. 'I suppose you wouldn't like to cook the meals? It would be a way of making an impression on him, you know.'

'I?' Martha's eyes opened wide with horror and astonishment. 'I cook in that awful kitchen? Oh, no, Sandy. You offered, so you can do it. I prefer to make my impression in other ways. And now I think you'd better get started or you're not going to have dinner ready for twelve-thirty.'

Martha was right. By the time Sandy had cleared away the breakfast dishes and washed them, found the meat and vegetables and prepared them, dealt with various interruptions from callers at the house, answered the telephone at least five times, it was almost noon.

But the meal was ready in time, and, a little flushed from the heat of the cooker, wishing she had had time to set the table more attractively and to see to her own appearance, Sandy served it dead on twelve-thirty. It was true that the mutton chops were a little tough, giving rise to the suspiciously sweet suggestion from Martha that perhaps they were of the stewing variety, and the marmalade pudding was a little soggy in the middle, but the men ate everything she put before them without complaint, and Johnnie endeared himself to her by saying kindly that he had enjoyed the food very much and hoped she would be cooking again while she stayed there.

It was then that disaster struck. Dermid, having missed Sandy's usually undivided attention that morning, and now finding himself ignored by the other three adults at the table as they discussed the merits of the local golf courses, began to bang on the table with his spoon and roar for some more pudding.

Martha turned to him and absently told him to be quiet, while she was obviously more interested in something Lymond was saying. The little boy ignored her and began to shout more loudly. Lymond turned on him and ordered him to shut up or be sent from the room. Flabbergasted at being spoken to in such an authoritative fashion, Dermid was silent for a moment, and glared at his uncle, who continued with what he had been saying.

But Dermid was not silent for long. Picking up his spoon again, he hurled it across the table at Lymond and cried,

'Horrid, horrid Uncle Lymond, I hate you! I don't think you're a knight in armour. You're just a horrid old uncle!'

The spoon only just missed Lymond. It fell behind his chair with a pinging sound on the stone floor. There was an awful silence as they all stared at Dermid. He looked anxiously at each one of them in turn, then burst into noisy sobs.

'Take him upstairs, Martha, and don't bring him to a meal until you're sure he can behave himself.'

Lymond's voice was quiet but authoritative. Martha looked sullen, as if she might object. Sandy caught her glance and shook her head from side to side. There was no use in defying Lymond at the moment, and she was relieved when Martha began to lift Dermid down from his chair. At once the child began to kick and squeal, pushing against his mother with all his might.

'Dermid, stop that, or I'll spank you!' This time Lymond's voice cracked like a whip. Dermid gave him a surprised but respectful glance and slid obediently off his chair.

'Lymond, he didn't mean it. He's only a little boy,' said Martha appealingly.

'I know he is,' Lymond replied pleasantly. 'But he has to learn how to behave. He's also a Caldwell and consequently hard to handle. You'll have to be firm with him. He'll get away with murder if you don't.'

Once again Martha looked as if she were going to object, but Lymond's hard steady stare was too much for her and with a sigh of frustration she left the room with Dermid.

A few minutes later both Lymond and Johnnie left the table and Sandy cleared it quickly, placing the dirty dishes in a pile on the draining board. The pile looked like a mountain to her and there were all the cooking utensils to be washed too. But before she did them she would have to go and comfort her cousin, for, if she were any judge of temperament, Martha would be weeping in her room.

She looked in the nursery to make sure Dermid was having his afternoon nap, then crossed the landing to Martha's room where she found her sitting on the edge of the bed, twisting a wisp of handkerchief between her fingers, while tears ran down her cheeks.

'Oh, Sandy,' she wailed, 'what am I going to do? Dermid has been so good this past week, since you came. I thought he'd got over having those tantrums. It would happen just when Lymond was beginning to show some interest in me, was actually talking to me and not ignoring me as he usually does. Now I'm right back where I started.'

'I don't agree,' said Sandy practically, going to sit beside her on the bed. 'Now we know why Dermid behaves badly.'

'Do we?' Martha sniffed and wiped the tears away from her eyes. 'Why does he?'

'He resents your attention being taken away from him by Lymond, and today he noticed it more because I was busy and not able to distract him . . .'

'I suppose you're right,' said Martha with a sigh. 'But how am I going to speak to Lymond? I only ever see him at mealtimes. You have to admit he isn't very sociable. Oh, Sandy, I don't seem to be getting anywhere with him. Have you been able to do anything?'

'No, not since that first day, and I told you about that.' Sandy paused, then added warily, 'Martha, you could be wasting your time staying here.'

'Oh, don't start that again!' Fresh tears started in Martha's eyes. 'He has to help Dermid, he must. You can see the child needs a father . . .' She couldn't say any more because sobs overwhelmed her.

'Well, crying isn't going to help,' said Sandy, getting to her feet. 'You'd better stop or you're going to look a mess for your outing this afternoon. What time are you going?'

Her words had the desired effect. Martha stopped crying and smiled through her tears. It was like seeing sunshine after rain, thought Sandy ruefully.

'Does that mean you'll look after Dermid for me?' asked Martha hopefully.

'Yes, it does. I don't suppose minding him will make much difference to what I have to do this afternoon.'

'Oh, thank you, darling. I do appreciate it,' said Martha,

sliding off the bed. 'Now what should I wear?' she added, other problems forgotten. 'The Irvines are picking me up at the end of the drive in about fifteen minutes, so I haven't much time to get ready.'

Sandy was washing up when Martha finally left. It took her another half hour to dry the dishes and put them way. Then she decided she had better clean the place a little.

She had just finished sweeping and mopping the floor, a job which took her far longer than she had expected and which made her feel quite hot and tired, when she heard Dermid shouting. She went to attend to him and had hardly got to the kitchen when Johnnie looked in.

'Time to collect the eggs,' he said with a grin. 'I'll show you where and how.'

They took Dermid along with them and he seemed quite happy to help until he dropped a couple of eggs and broke them. The little accident seemed to upset him more than it should, and Sandy decided that the incident with Lymond at dinner-time had shaken the little boy's faith in himself, and now he was afraid he'd be punished for everything he did.

Back in the house, busy placing eggs in boxes while Dermid played with his few toys, she was shocked to find that it was almost five o'clock, nearly time for high tea. At that moment the phone rang and she answered to hear an excited, laughing Martha saying that she had been invited out for the evening and asking Sandy to put Dermid to bed for her. Sandy replied that she would do that, rang off and hurried back to the kitchen.

She decided to feed Dermid and have her own tea with him, so that she could take him upstairs out of the way when Lymond came in for his meal. Even so she was pushed for time and the meal wasn't quite ready when he entered the kitchen. In response to her rather breathless explanation he gave her a derisive glance, but said nothing and went through to his study.

69

At last everything was ready and served and she was able to take Dermid for his bath. Bedtime, as usual, was prolonged by the child as he asked for one story after another, and it was a rather weary, dishevelled Sandy who eventually trailed downstairs to the kitchen to find Johnnie there washing up.

'Oh, thanks,' she said. 'You're an angel in disguise.'

'Not really,' he replied with a grin. 'I was detailed to do it by Lymond. Coming down to Creggan later?'

'I can't. Martha is out for the evening, so I'd better stay with Dermid since your mother is still resting. I'd like to have a look at the library. I have permission,' she said with a quick grin when he gave her a quizzical glance. 'Would you like to show me where it is?'

He agreed. The dishes were dried and put away and they went along the passage to the hall. Johnnie opened a door in the wall between the staircase and the front door and they stepped into a high-ceilinged room, made gloomy by the dark drooping curtains which were pulled across three full-length windows, two of which were at the front of the house and the third on the side wall.

Johnnie touched a switch on the wall beside the door, but light from the few bulbs in the two chandeliers did little to disperse the gloom, so Sandy went across to the nearest window and pulled back a curtain. She was immediately showered with sooty dirt and at the same time the curtain tore at the top and then hung raggedly from the wooden rings which attached it to the brass rod across the top of the window.

'A mess, isn't it?' remarked Johnnie.

She looked round and caught sight of her reflection in a huge mirror with a tarnished gilt frame. It hung above an elegant Adam fireplace, the white paint of which was grimy. On either side of the fireplace the walls were lined with shelves, crammed with books. Sandy guessed that before the room had been turned into a library, it must have been a lovely example of a gracious eighteenth-century drawing room.

'How could anyone let it get like this?' she exclaimed, crossing the room to gaze up at the books.

'The old man—I used to call him Uncle Gavin—was a recluse,' said Johnnie. 'He used to lock himself in here for days on end. Supposedly he was writing the history of Duncreggan, but he was also drinking himself silly.'

Sandy walked to the end of the room and carefully drew back the curtains from the window there. Western sunlight streamed into the room, lighting up the big desk which was in front of the window. The top of the desk was covered with papers. On the right was a silver tray on which there was a cut-glass decanter containing a small amount of golden-coloured liquor. On the left, in a silver frame, was a wedding photograph. It showed a man of about forty years of age; dark-haired, dark-browed and dark-eyed, wearing the uniform of an officer in the Scots Guards. Beside him, in a long white bridal gown, stood a woman who was much younger than he. She also had dark hair, but her eyes were light and her mouth had a merry mischievous quirk to it.

'What happened to him? Why did he become a recluse?' asked Sandy. 'Was it because he lost his wife?'

'Yes. She was drowned, out there, in the Firth.'

'Was she swimming at the time?'

'No.' Johnnie looked uncomfortable as he came across the room to look at the photograph. 'I've never seen this before. She was pretty, wasn't she? I know she was nearly twenty years younger than he was. Looking at her makes me think that perhaps there's some truth in the story after all.'

'What story? Oh, do tell me, Johnnie,' demanded Sandy, sensing a mystery.

'Well, when she was drowned she was sailing ...' he began.

71

'Alone?'

'No, with a man, on his yacht. The story goes that she was running away with him to Ireland, and the yacht went aground on one of the sandbanks in the Firth. There was a strong wind blowing and the boat keeled over violently, throwing them both overboard. With the tide running as it was they didn't stand a chance. Their bodies were washed up further down the coast.' Johnnie pointed to Gavin Caldwell. 'He couldn't take it. He was a proud devil and he couldn't bear for everyone to believe that his wife left him for another man . . .'

'Haven't you anything better to do than bore Sandy with local gossip?' asked a voice behind them.

They both turned quickly, a little guiltily. Lymond had entered the room and was standing in the middle of the floor, his hands in his trouser pockets. Judging by the frowning slant of his heavy eyebrows and the stern set of his mouth, he was not pleased to hear them discussing his parents.

'Sandy wanted to see the library,' muttered Johnnie, going red to the roots of his hair.

'And Nan would like to see you,' was the quiet, almost gentle retort. 'It's the monthly meeting of the Rural Institute tonight, and since she doesn't feel up to going she'd like you to take her apologies for absence as well as the minutes of the last meeting.'

'Oh, right. Excuse me, Sandy—duty calls.' Johnnie's grin was wide but slightly rueful as he went from the room, obviously glad to leave her to the not so tender mercies of Lymond Caldwell.

'He wasn't gossiping,' Sandy defended him. 'I wanted to know why your father was a recluse and why he had let everything deteriorate, and Johnnie was telling me. It's a sad story.'

'But hardly of interest to you,' he replied coolly.

'I can't agree. Anything which happened in the past is of

72

interest to me because it helps to explain the present.'

'Ah, yes, I'd forgotten. You're a budding historian and so you're interested in cause and effect,' he scoffed. He glanced round the room, made a grimace of dismay and went on slowly, 'I hadn't realised it was quite as bad as this. Maybe the whole lot should be burned, furniture, books, curtains . . .'

'Oh no, that would be sacrilege,' she protested, and as he gave her a surprised glance she rushed on to add, 'I mean, the books and the furniture could be cleaned up. Some of them must be valuable.'

'You think so?' He went across to peer up at the shelves, then swung round to look at her. 'How could I find out if they are?'

'I'm sure there must be someone at the Museum in Glasgow who could come and appraise the books for you, and anyone who knows about antique furniture could give you an opinion on those chairs and the desk.'

'The place would have to be cleaned before I could ask anyone to come and look at it,' he demurred.

'I could tidy the books, dust them and put them in order,' she offered, forgetful of the morning when he had tricked her into offering to do Nan's work.

He leaned his shoulders against the elegant mantelpiece, thrust his hands in his pockets again and gave her an underbrowed glance.

'You seem to be full of offers to do good,' he jibed softly. 'And I haven't thanked you yet for helping today. You did far better than I expected you would.'

Don't let such faint praise go to your head, Sandy warned herself. He'll be trapping you into doing more if you're not careful.

'Thank you,' she replied sedately. 'Perhaps now you won't be so quick to assume that because a woman has abilities in other directions she is not capable of doing work which has been considered hers since the beginning of time.'

73

There was that tell-tale twitch at the corner of his mouth, but his eyes remained blank.

'You don't like me, do you?' he accused suddenly.

Not having any answer ready, remembering belatedly that she should be making diplomatic approaches to him about Dermid, Sandy could only say defensively,

'I hardly know you well enough to come to a decision about you.'

'Oh, very skilful,' he jeered. 'But you don't deceive me. You don't like me. You think I'm overbearing, cynical and possibly mean.'

'I ... er ... Yes, I do,' she flashed, recovering her spirit. 'And I know you disapprove of me as much as you do of Martha.'

'What makes you think that?'

'The way you make fun of me all the time. That shows you're hostile to me.'

'Well, that's a slant I haven't heard before,' he mocked. 'Tell me, what did you expect when you came here? An amorous adventure, perhaps, with a Scottish laird?'

'Oh!' gasped Sandy, wondering how and why the situation had developed as it had; why every time she met him she found herself crossing swords with him in some way when her intentions were always the opposite. 'Don't be so silly,' she went on scornfully. 'I didn't expect anything like that. I'm not one of those silly women who go around seeing every man as a ... as a ...'

'As a sex object, I believe the current phrase is,' he supplied for her with a tantalising grin. 'Then how do you see men from that lofty intellectual perch of yours? Do you see us as Martha does? As providers of bed and board, as protectors from the discomforts of reality, possibly as scapegoats for your own failings?'

'No, I don't,' she replied indignantly, secretly horrified by the impression he had of Martha. 'I see men as other

74

persons, as people I can talk to about mutual interests, and I hope they see me in the same way.'

His dark glance flicked over her slim figure, outlined by a close-fitting scooped-necked cotton sweater and close-fitting jeans which flared out gradually to fullness in the legs.

'Possibly some men do see you like that,' he murmured, and there was a glint of admiration in his eyes as they strayed back slowly to her face.

'But you don't,' she accused, disturbed by that glint.

'Not all the time,' he replied coolly. 'I like and enjoy the differences women offer and don't care much for the theory that sexes are equal.'

'That is very obvious,' she said flatly, spoiling for a fight, and felt a strange sense of defeat when he merely grinned at her as he moved away from the fireplace on his way to the door.

'Could I talk to you about Dermid?' she asked, tentatively following him.

He swung round suddenly to face her, forcing her to stop abruptly or she might have walked into him.

'A mutual interest?' he inquired mockingly, and, slightly confused at finding herself so close to him, Sandy stepped back a pace. 'What about Dermid?' he prompted.

'Please don't think too badly of him because of the way he behaved at the table today. You see, he's confused by you,' she said earnestly.

'Why is that?' he demanded.

'I think it's because although you look like his father you don't behave like him,' she ventured.

He folded his arms across his chest and his eyes narrowed thoughtfully.

'That could be,' he agreed, then grinned mischievously and she saw a sudden resemblance to the young woman in the photograph on the desk. 'He's not the first person to be confused by Crawford's and my likeness to each other. We used to play on it at times.' The grin faded and he frowned. 'Did Martha ask you to put in a word for the child because I threatened to spank him?'

'No, but she is worried about his tantrums. She knows he needs a father and . . .' Sandy broke off because of the ironical glance he gave her. 'She would like him to grow up here and go eventually to the same school you and your brother went to. Crawford didn't leave her any money, and although she has a little annuity of her own left to her by her parents, it isn't enough, you see, to cover the cost of such an education.'

He stared at her, obviously weighing what she had said in his mind. Then he asked slowly,

'Are you sure that's all she wants?'

'Yes,' she answered, saw his eyebrows go up in disbelief, remembered the conversation she had had with Martha on the sands and the letter 'L', and added reluctantly, 'No, I'm not sure.'

'I thought you mightn't be,' he murmured drily. 'Any idea where she is this evening?'

'She phoned to say she had been invited out for the evening. She went to play golf with the Irvines this afternoon at Kirkton.'

'I see. She couldn't have done that if you hadn't been here, because both Johnnie and I draw the line at baby-sitting and Nan isn't always available. I'm beginning to realise that your cousin is pretty good at cool, long-range planning, a real strategist. I think my father might have approved of her,' he observed rather obscurely. 'I'll leave you now to get on with your search for the history of Duncreggan while I go and try to balance the accounts. Good hunting, and let me know what you think of it, if you find it.'

Alone in the dust-laden room, Sandy turned back to the big desk. There were three drawers in it and they were all full of folders, each one crammed with sheets of paper covered in fine neat writing. A drunken recluse Gavin Caldwell might have become in his later years, but the inner man, the creative man, had remained disciplined to the end, and every folder was labelled neatly and arranged in the drawers in numerical order so that the first one she lifted out was the introduction to the history.

Excited by what she had found, Sandy took the first folder up to her room and was soon absorbed in reading what had been written there about the origins of the settlement known as Duncreggan.

Next day Nan was back to normal. Since Martha seemed disposed to sleep in after her late night, Sandy once again took charge of Dermid and they went as usual to the beach. Back to the house they went at dinner-time, and after giving Dermid his meal in the nursery Sandy settled down to continue reading Gavin Caldwell's history.

She was not left in peace long, for Martha came in and began at once to talk about the golf she had enjoyed the previous day.

'Guess who turned up, just as we got back to the club house?'

'I haven't the slightest idea,' said Sandy.

'Bill. Bill Lindsay,' replied Martha. She was lying prone on Sandy's bed. Her shapely legs were bent up and swinging from the knee and she was munching an apple. 'Anyway, to cut a long story short, he invited me out to dinner with him, and afterwards we went back to Brookfield, the house on the bay. It's gorgeous, a great improvement on this place.'

'Did his sister go with you to dinner?'

'Oh, no, but she was at the house, on her best behaviour, in front of her mother.' Martha laughed at little. 'In fact she was very friendly, but she said the oddest things, Sandy. She said I was lucky to have met the Caldwell brothers separately. What do you think of that?'

'Perhaps she used to know them when she was younger

and was one of the people they confused by their likeness to each other. When I was telling Lymond that Dermid was confused because he looks like Crawford, but doesn't behave like him, he told me he and Crawford used to play tricks on people by pretending to be each other. I expect it's something twins often do.'

'Yes, I suppose so. It could have been that, because later she asked me if I was sure I'd married Crawford and not Lymond. It gave me a nasty jolt, and I still have this funny feeling she doesn't like me, and it isn't because my last name is now Caldwell. What are you reading?'

'A history of Duncreggan written by Gavin Caldwell. It's very interesting and exciting. Did you know that there's a possibility this is the site of a Dark Ages fort which was one of the last strongholds to resist the Anglo-Saxons in the sixth century? It might have been built by King Urbgen or Urien of Rheged. He ruled over a kingdom which stretched from south of Carlisle, through Dumfriesshire into Galloway as far as Stranraer.'

'When?' murmured Martha, unsuccessfully trying to stifle a yawn.

'About the time of the mythical King Arthur. In fact some of the stories about King Urbgen's stand against the Anglo-Saxons may have contributed to the myth.'

'Oh, really. Do you mean the King Arthur in the musical play Camelot?' asked Martha, showing an interest now she had recognised a name.

'Yes, that king,' replied Sandy. 'Gavin Caldwell was trying to prove his theory by excavating and he actually found some artefacts—a brooch of Celtic design and some ingot moulds. I wonder where he put them?'

'Nan might know,' drawled Martha. 'He must have been a real tartar to live with. Have you heard what happened to his wife?'

'Yes, Johnnie told me last night. Do you think there's any

truth in the story that she was running away with another man?'

'I know it's true. Crawford told me,' said Martha flatly.

'Did he tell you why she was running away?'

'No. I just guessed she'd found someone she liked better.' Martha shrugged it off. 'It happens all the time, ducky.'

'I suppose it does,' murmured Sandy musingly. 'She was responsible for so much which happened afterwards,' she muttered more to herself than to Martha.

'What do you mean?' asked Martha, rolling on to her back and stretching luxuriously like a pet cat.

'Cause and effect,' replied Sandy. 'It's what history is all about. If Phillida Caldwell hadn't been drowned while sailing with another man, her husband might not have become a recluse. Consequently he might not have quarrelled with his sons and let this place deteriorate.'

'How awful!' exclaimed Martha, sitting up and shuddering. 'If I thought like that, looked ahead to the possible consequences of my actions, I'd never do anything. You really think she was to blame for the old man quarrelling with Crawford and telling him not to come back here?'

'Not to blame exactly, but it's possible he would not have been so bad-tempered, and it's also possible that Crawford and Lymond would have been different if their mother had stayed with them. Her behaviour must have affected them, you know.'

'I suppose so,' murmured Martha.

'Do you know what the quarrel was about?'

'Only vaguely. Crawford was very defensive about it, felt he had been wronged. He said his father found out about something he had done years ago, before Lymond left home, and was furious about it. I've a feeling Lymond was involved. But what can it matter now? It happened over twelve years ago. The old man has gone, Crawford has gone, and now there are only Lymond and Dermid. Did Lymond say anything to you last night about Dermid's future?'

79

'Not until I opened the subject. I told him what you want for the boy, since you don't seem to be able to do that for yourself,' replied Sandy rather sharply.

'Good for you,' said Martha eagerly. 'Go on, Sandy. What did he say? Did he say he'd finance Dermid's education?'

'No. He just asked me if I was sure that was all you wanted and I had to tell him I wasn't sure. Martha, I wish you'd be more direct with him and discuss Dermid's future with him yourself. I won't be here much longer. He invited me to stay for only two weeks, remember, and that time is up on Wednesday.'

'You could stay longer,' said Martha. 'I'm sure he won't mind really.'

'But I will mind.'

Martha looked suddenly troubled and tears brimmed in her eyes, so that Sandy felt mean and disloyal.

'Perhaps if he knew what else it is you want he could come to a decision more quickly,' she persisted. 'Martha, is the financing of Dermid's education all you want?'

Martha traced the pattern of a flower on her gaily printed dress with a pointed fingernail. That faintly provocative smile was hovering about her mouth again, as if she had a secret which gave her great pleasure.

'No, it isn't all I want, but if you don't mind I'm not going to tell you just yet exactly what I'm after. You see, love, I'm afraid that if I tell anyone about it, it might not happen. And I do want it to happen. You know the feeling?'

'Yes,' sighed Sandy. 'I know the feeling, but . . .'

'Bear with me, love, please,' pleaded Martha. 'And thanks for talking to Lymond. I've been thinking you could be right about Phillida's behaviour having an effect on the twins. It could be why they both had the reputation of loving women and leaving them.'

'Had they?' exclaimed Sandy.

'Yes, and I know Crawford was like that until he met me,'

said Martha, rising to her feet and walking to the door with a seductive swagger of her hips.

'How did you manage to stop him from leaving you?' asked Sandy, and Martha turned in the doorway, to give her a long pitying look.

'You may have a degree, darling, but you don't know much about things that matter, do you?' she taunted. 'That's another thing I'd better not tell you, but it worked with him.'

'But it isn't working with his brother,' remarked Sandy softly, watching closely for reaction.

It came. Martha frowned and bit her lip.

'No,' she admitted reluctantly. 'At least it hasn't yet.' Then she smiled, her lovely sunny smile. 'It sounds as if Dermid is awake again. Time to go down to the beach. Thank heavens the weather is keeping fine.'

Later, when the sun was low and shadows were beginning to gather in the hollows of the hills, when the moon hung like a golden medallion in an ice-green sky and a faint breeze rustled the trees and grass, Sandy perched on the let-down hood of Ron Carson's two-seater sports car as it swept down into the village of Creggan.

The tide was going out. Mudbanks were appearing, looking like sleek stranded whales. Between them the rapidly narrowing channel of water was shimmering with silver-dappled rosy light as the sun sank and flushed the whole of the western sky with crimson.

Ron parked the car on the strip of grass between the road and the narrow shore. With him and Johnnie, Sandy crossed the road to the hotel, a plain-fronted four-square building, where they were going to meet some more of the young people who came every year to the village to stay with their parents in rented holiday homes, or who lived locally and were home for the summer holidays from universities and schools. Nan had agreed to look after Dermid.

They entered the lounge of the hotel. It was full, but not

as full as the bar-room beyond, where groups of people were seated round tables drinking beer and chattering.

Room was made for the newcomers at one of the tables, Sandy was introduced and more beer was ordered.

'Look who's in the corner,' Johnnie whispered in her ear, and she saw that Martha was seated at a table with several other people, one of whom was Bill Lindsay.

'She said she was going to walk over to see the end of the race,' explained Sandy.

'And I can guess who was in the lead in that race—Bill Lindsay. Hey, Ron, who's the woman sitting next to the vice-commodore over there?'

Ron glanced over.

'His sister, of course—you know, the one who ...' He broke off as someone touched his arm and passed him some beer. When he turned back to Johnnie he had apparently forgotten about Helen Lindsay, for he said, 'Have you seen who's serving behind the bar tonight? Your little blonde friend. Wonder if she'll be at the dance after closing time.'

'I can always hope,' said Johnnie.

Half an hour later they were just thinking of leaving to go along to the dance which was taking place in the village hall, when Ron leaned towards Johnnie and said rather facetiously,

'Looks as if you've had it with the blonde barmaid, Johnnie. A relative of yours is doing a good line over there at the bar.'

Sandy looked, as Johnnie did, and felt herself tingle with surprise. Lymond was leaning against the bar. He was wearing the jacket of fine grey tweed he had worn the day he had met her in Dumfries, over a black high-necked sweater and black trousers. With his rough black hair and pale aquiline face he looked aloof and distinguished, somehow out of place among the holidaymakers in their many-coloured clothes.

Like a black knight at a tournament. The thought flashed

through Sandy's mind just as Johnnie muttered,

'I can guess why he's here, too. Surprising what a little competition will do,' and in answer to Ron's query he jerked his head in the direction of the corner where Martha was sitting with Bill Lindsay.

At that moment Lymond half turned and glanced in that direction too, so Sandy looked as well. Martha, in high spirits, was telling a story, obviously disregarding Lymond's presence in the room. On the other hand Helen Lindsay, her blue eyes bright and startled in a paper-white face, was staring at Lymond as if she had seen a ghost.

Feeling a little as if she had been spying on Helen in an unguarded moment, Sandy looked away, only to find that Lymond was watching herself. She nodded a little shyly at him, furious at feeling the colour run up under her fair skin. He nodded back and just then Ron suggested they leave and go to the dance.

They all went into the soft still air, to find a dark-blue sky in which pin-points of stars twinkled about the moon, which was now a silver medallion hanging above the sea.

Again Sandy sat on the collapsed roof of the car as it sped along the road to the village hall, from which the sound of music was already twanging and thumping.

In the hall they soon joined in the dancing to the noisy beat of a youthful rock group on the stage. Dancing was a form of escape, thought Sandy as she twirled and twisted about, as well as being a form of self-expression. Tensions were released and problems were forgotten in rhythmical exercise.

The music stopped. She collapsed on to one of the chairs arranged against the wall. Ron sat down beside her and Johnnie came to stand in front of them. All about them there was the noise of many voices.

Ron leaned forward, peering towards the door. He glanced up at Johnnie and said with a grin,

'Don't look now, but she's come, with him.'

'Who?' Johnnie demanded, swinging round to look. Sandy looked, fully expecting to see Martha with Lymond. But instead of her cousin's red-gold head she saw the fall of smooth blonde hair. He was with the barmaid.

'Doesn't waste much time, does he?' scoffed Ron, watching Johnnie's black scowl. 'You could use him as a way of getting an introduction to her, though.'

'How?' growled Johnnie.

'In one of those old-style dances we're bound to have sooner or later, you know, the change-partners kind, to a slow country waltz.'

He was right, because in few minutes the rock group's place was taken by a Scottish country dance band complete with fiddler and accordionist, and the leader announced that the first dance tune played would be a country-style waltz and anyone who hadn't a partner could cut in on a couple that was dancing.

'Now's your chance, lad,' Ron urged Johnnie with a grin. 'Come on, Sandy, have a go at this with me.'

They circled round the room and Ron kept up a running commentary on all that was happening.

'He's done it!' he crowed at last. 'Johnnie cut in and Lymond gave up without a fight. I expect you've heard about the antics he and his twin brother used to get up to when they came to these dances years ago?'

'No, I haven't. Tell me about them,' said Sandy rather breathlessly. Slow the country waltz might be called, but the strict rhythm and endless whirling soon began to have their effect on leg muscles and breathing.

'My sister Jean—she's married now and has a couple of bairns—says the twins were devils,' said Ron. 'Once she went to a dance with Lymond and was taken home by Crawford, but she didn't know they'd done a swap on her until a week later, when the girl Lymond had taken home told her. They were always doing it. In the end it led to trouble, as you might expect.'

'What sort of trouble?' asked Sandy.

'Och, one of them was blamed for doing something the other had done, that sort of trouble, and later the old man, their father, found out . . .'

'Excuse me. Mind if I cut in, Ron?' The voice was Lymond's and he was there cool and unsmiling, almost as if he had guessed that Ron was about to tell her something which he did not want her to know, just as he had appeared in the library when Johnnie had been telling her about Phillida Caldwell.

'I might have guessed I'd be hoist by my own petard,' said Ron with his cheerful grin. 'See you later, Sandy,' he added, also giving up without a struggle; already his eyes were searching among the crowd of local girls chatting and giggling together by the wall.

It was strange how easily she had been able to dance with Ron, but now, with one of Lymond's hands on her waist and his other holding hers in a firm cool clasp, she felt stiff and awkward.

Too much to hope that he hadn't noticed.

'You seem uncomfortable,' he remarked.

'I feel very warm in here. It's so crowded.'

'Then let's take a walk outside to cool off,' he suggested, and guided her to the edge of the floor right beside the chair where she had left her cardigan.

Sandy hesitated, glancing round. But Johnnie had no eyes for anyone but the blonde barmaid, and Ron was engrossed in his new partner, a girl of eighteen or so with a mop of black curls.

She looked back at Lymond. He had been watching her, apparently reading her thoughts with gypsy-like insight.

'Their present partners are much more to their taste than you'll ever be,' he drawled.

'Oh, that isn't a very nice thing to say,' she objected, wondering how he knew she had often been in this position at dances when the young men who had found her a useful and practical friend in the lecture hall or on a field trip had shown they preferred prettier, more frivolous companions on the dance floor.

'I meant it as a compliment,' he replied. 'Just now they're more interested in outward show than in substance, in what a woman appears to be rather than in what she is. You're too serious and possibly too innocent to appeal to them tonight, when all they want is some fun.'

'How do you know that's all they want?' she challenged.

He lifted his shoulders in a shrug and his smile flickered briefly, attractively.

'Because I used to come to these dances some twelve years ago for that reason,' he drawled. 'Are you going to come outside with me to walk in the moonlight and discuss our mutual interests?'

Now she was sure he was mocking her. She studied his face warily. He returned her gaze without a flicker of expression.

'What mutual interests do you and I have?' she parried. A new strange sense, which she seemed to have developed only since she had met him, was warning her that it would be dangerous for her to walk with him in the moonlight.

'Dermid's future, Martha's happiness. I've a few questions to ask to which you might know the answers. I might even ask your advice,' he said softly. 'Coming?'

CHAPTER FOUR

TAKING up her cardigan from the chair and slinging it round her shoulders, Sandy went with Lymond, as he must have known she would when he suggested that they discuss Dermid's future and Martha's happiness. For wasn't that her role at present, to act as go-between? That he regarded her as such was obvious, otherwise he would not have made such a calculated effort to get her to himself for a short while.

Stepping from the crowded noisy hall into the soft moonlit night was like stepping into a world of black and white enchantment. The path they trod glittered with sparks as the granite chips from which it was made caught the pale light and flashed it back. Among the gaunt silhouettes of pine trees the white walls of a house shone with a ghostly gleam. Down in the estuary silvery dazzle danced on water which was briefly ruffled by a faint night breeze, and beyond it the curved hills hunched black shoulders against the moon-bleached sky.

A perfect night for lovers, thought Sandy, then grinned at her unoriginal thought as the voice of the aloof man walking beside her brought her down to earth.

'How long has Martha known Bill Lindsay?'

So Johnnie had not been off course when he had implied that it was competition which had brought the rather reclusive Lymond out tonight to socialise in the village pub. Perhaps he had heard a rumour that Martha had been seen several times with the Lindsays and had come to find if there was any truth in it.

'I'm not sure. She met him before I came, I think, possibly at the yacht club when Johnnie took her there. Dermid plays with the Lindsay children nearly every day at the beach and sometimes Bill comes there.' She saw suddenly how that might look to him, and rushed on to defend her cousin. 'I shouldn't worry about it if I were you. Martha likes to have a lot of friends. She's very gregarious and I think she finds . . .' She broke off, aware that she had been about to say something which might seem unappreciative of his hospitality and give him good cause to tell her that no one was asking Martha to extend her stay at Duncreggan.

'So I'd noticed,' he observed drily. 'But when I saw her

going off in Bill's car tonight I had to admit to feeling surprised that she'd found friends in that quarter.'

'Because of the feud?' she asked.

'What feud?' he demanded.

'Nan told me about it. There was a feud between the Caldwells and Lindsays at one time and the two families used to fight over land claims and cattle. Surely you don't continue with it now?'

'I should have guessed you'd lap up all those tales about our barbaric ancestors,' he said with a laugh. 'Now we don't fight over land and cattle. We're much more subtle.'

'In what way?'

'Well, for instance, when Helen Lindsay began to show too much of an interest in Crawford a few years ago, the affair was nipped in the bud by her mother.'

'Oh, did she want to marry him?' exclaimed Sandy brightly, as another puzzle seemed to solve itself satisfactorily. 'I suppose that's why she acted so strangely when Bill introduced her to Martha. I suppose she felt that perhaps Martha had succeeded where she had failed. And then she stared at you in the pub as if she'd seen a ghost.'

'Did she? I didn't notice. She always had difficulty in telling Crawford and me apart,' he replied indifferently.

'Like several other young women, if there's any truth in what I heard tonight,' she teased.

'You heard it from Jean Carson's younger brother, I've no doubt,' he said with a wicked chuckle. 'Poor Jean, she never forgave us.'

'Well, you were rather unkind, playing tricks like that.'

'We used to do it for fun, not to hurt,' he said slowly. 'And it was only when we grew up that it began to have unpleasant repercussions.'

'And you were blamed for doing something Crawford had done,' she murmured, hardly realising that she had spoken a thought aloud.

Lymond stopped suddenly in his tracks and turned on

88

her. He grasped one of her arms and jerked her round to face him. Moonlight fell directly on her face, revealing her startled expression. His face was half in shadow, half in light, a black and white mask.

'Who told you that?' he rapped.

'No one told me. Ron said he'd heard a rumour that possibly one of you had been blamed for doing something the other had done. I guessed you were the one who was blamed.'

'And what led you to that assumption?' Although his voice was still cool and slightly ironic, she knew he was angry by the way his fingers gripped her arm.

'I put two and two together,' she retorted lightly, hoping to divert his anger. But his grip did not relax until she gasped, 'You . . . you're hurting my arm!'

He let go of her immediately and she heard his breath hiss between his teeth in a sigh of exasperation.

'Would you mind telling me what your two and two are?' he asked in a cold taut voice.

'Only what I've heard about Crawford from Martha and Nan and what I've learned about you from staying in your house.'

He was startled, she could see, because he turned his head sharply to look at her and his shoulders stiffened.

'It looks as if I'll have to be more careful about what I do and what I say while you're at Duncreggan,' he said between set teeth. 'I hadn't realised that a historian is a sort of detective. But you needn't think you're going to open any cupboard doors and pull out any family skeletons. There's been too much of this putting two and two together by the gossips of this district and coming up with five. That's how they managed to destroy my father's peace of mind one way and another, so you won't do any more ferreting for information about me or Crawford while you're here. Do I make myself clear?'

Sandy stood still, feeling anger rise warmly within her.

89

She was angry with herself because all unwittingly she had laid herself open to criticism and had come up against the unyielding Caldwell pride.

'Perfectly clear,' she retorted. 'But I haven't been ferreting. I can't help it if people talk about you and your family.'

'No, but you can stop trying to deduce from what you hear,' he snapped back. 'You may find it necessary to know about the past so that you can understand what's happening in the present, but I prefer to close the door on it. I've had to do that in order to rescue Duncreggan and make it a productive and profitable farm, so that when the next Caldwell comes along there'll be more for him to inherit than a mouldy broken-down house, a tottering castle, fields rank with weeds and a fistful of bad debts. Glooming over the past, cutting himself off from the present as my father did, produced precisely nothing.'

'Oh, I can't agree. It produced his history, which seems to be the work of a very scholarly man. But perhaps you'd prefer to burn it with the books, the curtains and the furniture,' she retaliated, still furious. 'Oh, Lymond, I understand what you're trying to do, but can't you see that what happened in the past made you what you are, a person who is determined to strive and do better for future generations. You've learned from your father's mistakes, and that's how it should be.'

Her words rang out earnestly and seemed to hang in the short silence which followed them.

'You sound as if you care about what I'm trying to do,' said Lymond slowly, with a touch of amazement.

'I do, I do care,' she assured him sincerely, and there was another brief breathless silence. Then to her surprise he laughed.

'This is the first time I've taken a walk with a woman in the moonlight and spent the time arguing with her,' he drawled.

'There wouldn't have been any argument if you hadn't

taken offence because I'd concluded you took the blame for something your brother had done,' she said. 'I wouldn't be surprised if you often took the blame for him and were proud of yourself for doing it, so that you're a little shattered now to learn that someone has guessed at the truth . . .'

'Stop it, stop it.' He was half laughing as he took hold of her arms and shook her to make her stop. 'Can't you see you're destroying my conviction that I was doing the right thing by keeping quiet whenever I was blamed?'

'But it seems awful to me that someone like you should be blamed for something which was done by someone like Crawford,' she protested.

'Someone like me, someone like Crawford,' he mocked her. 'We were cast in the same mould, tarred with the same brush. There wasn't much to choose between us.'

'There was enough,' she insisted. 'And in recent years there must have been more. Different experiences made you develop differently.' She wished she could ask him what Crawford had done, but knew he would accuse her of ferreting if she did.

'Perhaps,' he said non-committally. He was still holding her arms and it struck her that he was standing very still as he watched her. 'But neither of us would have ever wasted an opportunity like this,' he added softly.

He moved suddenly out of that hovering stillness, swooped like a hawk on its prey. His mouth claimed hers in a hard stifling kiss, but as she felt his hands slide up her arms to take a closer hold of her she pulled away and, turning, ran down the path towards the lights and the music.

She ran with her hand to her mouth, and her heart felt as if it would burst. She didn't know why she was running. There was just an instinctive urge to escape, before it was too late, from someone who was capable of taking over both her mind and her body, who could become more important to her than any other person, more important even than herself.

Outside the door of the village hall she paused to catch her breath and calm herself. With her hands she flattened her hair, stroking it down over her head, smoothing it so that it lay tidily on her shoulders. It wouldn't do to look too flushed and dishevelled, for both Johnnie and Ron had sharp eyes and weren't above making some derisive comment. For a moment she listened intently, trying to detect the sound of footsteps which might have followed her down the path, but the sound of the music coming from the hall made it impossible to tell whether Lymond was following her or not.

Bracing herself, she pushed open the door and entered the noise-filled dancing room. To find Johnnie or Ron was her one desire; to be with them or among their friends when Lymond returned to the hall, if he returned. Only in that way would she feel safe.

But it was difficult to see whether either of them was still there among the whirling crowd. Then she spotted one of the girls who had been with the group at the pub. She sidled round to her, leaned close and said as loudly as she could, so as to be heard above the noise,

'Have you seen Ron or Johnnie?'

The girl shook her head and smiled.

'Och, they've gone away to Kirkton. They left about fifteen minutes ago. They looked for you and couldn't find you. Johnnie thought you might be with his cousin Lymond, and said to tell you, if you came back, where he'd gone.'

'Oh, thank you, thanks very much.'

Back to the door Sandy struggled and out into the moonlight again. Lymond hadn't come after her, at least she couldn't see him. She stood hesitantly, wondering what to do. She could either walk back to Duncreggan round by the road, or she could go over the hill, a way as yet unknown to her, but which tempted her on that clear night.

The path went up, as far as she could remember from Martha's description, from a point where the village road ended, so turning away from the hall she made her way down to the road and began to walk to the far end of the village.

Past the cottages where oblongs of yellow and rosy light glowed she went, past the hotel, now quiet and dim, past the yacht club, past the village shop. A few more houses and the road stopped abruptly, giving way to rough grass.

There seemed to be a path of sorts, so she set off along it. The moon had moved along the sky and was now sliding down towards the west. Taking her bearings from it, she decided that Duncreggan should lie in the opposite direction, to the east, yet the path seemed to be going south.

Perhaps it turned east further along, she comforted herself, and walked on, enjoying the smell of the sea, the touch of soft air on her face, and the silvery radiance of the moon.

It was quiet, so quiet she could hear the sucking, bubbling noise of water swirling among the rocks which edged the estuary to her right. The pathway narrowed, bushes crowded about her. She guessed they were mostly hawthorn and briar rose, thick with thorns. Their ragged branches seemed to reach out with witchlike claws to snatch at her cardigan. Now the water noises seemed nearer and had a sinister sound. She could no longer see where she was going because the bushes blotted out the moonlight. Fear of the unknown and the unseen arose within her, making her skin clammy and her throat dry.

Behind her something crackled, a twig snapping, perhaps. But what had made it snap? She whirled round, saw a shadow looming and cried out, 'Who's there?'

'Sandy?' The voice was Lymond's, raised in query. 'Where are you going?'

The shadow came nearer, took on substance. Reaction set in as she recognised him, and she began to shake.

'What's the matter?' he asked.

'I didn't hear you coming,' she stuttered. 'Oh, you gave me a terrible fright!'

The shaking wouldn't stop. He came right up to her and again she felt his hands on her arms.

'Don't touch me,' she stammered through chattering teeth.

He ignored her protest, pulled her against him and held her closely.

'I didn't mean to frighten you. I was on the other path, on my way home, when I saw you come this way. Now calm down, lass, there's nothing to be afraid of.' The firmness of his arms, the warmth of his body, the use of the homely word 'lass' and the undercurrent of laughter in his voice all combined to reassure her, and slowly the shaking stopped.

'We'll go back to Duncreggan together,' he went on quietly. 'You took the wrong path. If you'd continued along this one you'd have come out on the sands, and at this stage of the tide that would have done you no good at all.'

Realising suddenly how much she was enjoying being held by him and how comforting it was to lean against his warmth and strength, Sandy stiffened and tried to move away. At once he released her.

'Feeling all right now?' he asked.

'Yes, thank you. I don't know what came over me. I don't usually take fright like that.'

'Possibly because you're not used to being alone in the country at night. Even by moonlight, perhaps more so by moonlight, it's easy to let your imagination get the better of you,' he said with such insight into her recent behaviour that she was alarmed.

'How do you know that's what happened?' she gasped.

'Do you think you're the only person to whom it's happened?' he scoffed. 'Nan would tell you it was your instinct warning you of danger, and this time she would

94

be right. The sands are gluey in this area, and you might have stepped into a bad patch and been sucked down.'

'Quicksands?' she almost shrieked, and felt her hair rise on her neck.

'Yes. Are you recovered enough to go back to the other path now?'

'Yes, thank you. That's the second time you've rescued me.'

'Is it?'

'Yes. Remember when I was locked in the castle?'

'I remember.'

They went back along the path towards the village.

'The path to Duncreggan over the hill comes out in a lane behind the shop,' explained Lymond, and soon they were walking up that lane which angled steeply up the hillside. In the bright light of the moon Sandy could see the shapes of new bungalows in the process of being built and guessed it was the land which Lymond had sold to Ron Carson's father for development.

'I suppose Johnnie and Ron had left the dance when you got back to the hall,' said Lymond casually, as the lane became a track which twisted upwards through a copse of softly whispering pine trees.

'Yes. They've gone to Kirkton, so I thought I'd try and find my own way back.'

'It isn't safe to come this way, either, unless you know it well. You could wander round in circles on this hill. Every clump of trees, every outcrop of rock, every whinbush looks the same as the last one,' he said. 'You know, for a person who claims to be independent and capable you take fright very easily. Was that what happened when I kissed you? Was that why you ran away?'

'No,' she lied. 'I just didn't like your assuming you could kiss me. Why did you?'

'I told you, it was too good an opportunity to miss. And it's time someone treated you as the woman you are and not as the sexless object you seem to think you are. The dress makes a difference, too. You should wear one more often.'

Although his scoffing remarks roused her, Sandy saved her breath for climbing the hill. At last they reached the top, a craggy ridge crowned with whin and bracken. They paused to rest and look back at the view of moon-shot glimmering mudbanks beyond which the water of the Firth moved perpetually, now in moonlight, now in darkness. Far away on an unseen horizon a white light flashed regularly, presumably from a lighthouse marking a dangerous point of land.

' "How sweet the moonlight sleeps upon this bank," ' Lymond quoted suddenly, surprising her. 'I forget the rest of it. You're nearer to your schooldays than I am. Did you ever read *The Merchant of Venice*? Do you remember the rest?'

'Yes, I read the play at school, and I remember the scene between Jessica and Lorenzo very well, but the speech I like best is Jessica's when she goes one better than Lorenzo and says:

> "In such a night
> Did young Lorenzo swear he loved her well,
> Stealing her soul with many vows of faith
> And ne'er a true one . . ." '

Sandy spoke the words drily and he laughed appreciatively.

'I think I get the message,' he said. 'You're letting me know you're not to be led astray in the moonlight by soft words and kisses. Don't worry, you're quite safe. I shan't swear I love you, but I might just kiss you again.'

She stepped back quickly to avoid him, and her heel turned on a loose stone. She lost her balance, would have fallen backwards into the mass of bracken and whinbushes which filled the hollow behind her if Lymond had not grabbed her and held her steady, his hands at her waist.

'Rescue number three,' he mocked. 'It's getting to be a habit. But you over-reacted. I didn't say I was going to kiss you again, *now*. Watch your step as we go on. There are many loose stones on the way and I wouldn't like you to sprain an ankle.'

They turned their backs on the moon and walked down the other side of the hill in silence, seeing their shadows move jerkily before them across moon-silvered fronds of waist-high bracken.

By now Sandy was in such a state of confusion that she could not have talked sensibly anyway. Walking back to Duncreggan by moonlight with Lymond Caldwell was proving to be an experience which was upsetting her equilibrium in more ways than one. She had a feeling that after this hour of moon-madness she would never be the same again.

'What happens to you when the summer is over and October comes?' he asked suddenly, as if he had been thinking about her.

'I'm going back to university to take a postgraduate degree.'

'So you're not playing at being an intellectual just to fill in time until you get married, you're really interested,' he observed.

'Yes, I am. I'd like to work in the archaeology department of a museum when I've finished studying,' she said.

'Haven't you any plans to set up house with someone, possibly have children?' he inquired.

'Not yet, not for years and years, and then only if I meet the right person.'

'Who will of course be someone with whom you'll have mutual interests such as arrowheads, pottery urns and burial chambers,' he scoffed softly, revealing that he had more knowledge about archaeology than he usually let on. 'I gather you haven't met him yet.'

Sandy thought of Derek, of his thin ascetic face, his

perpetually furrowed brow and his wispy fair hair.

'I believe I might have met him,' she answered seriously. 'I hope to find out at the end of the summer. He's away just now.'

'And I suppose you're trying to find out if absence from him has made your heart grow fonder or whether the reverse will happen?' he said in the same lightly derisive way.

'How did you know that's what I'm doing?' she demanded.

'It was a method I used myself once.'

'And did it work? Did you find out?'

'I found that once out of my sight she was out of my mind and that there were many more flowers waiting around to be picked.' Now there was a suggestion of cynicism in his voice.

'Did you pick any of them?'

'Yes, but not to keep.'

'Do you think you'll ever find one you'd like to keep?'

Only while under the spell of moon magic would she have dared to ask such a personal question, thought Sandy.

'I believe I may have done,' he replied in deliberate mockery of the way she had answered him. 'Maybe by the end of the summer I'll know.'

Martha. Could he be thinking of Martha? How could she find out without the appearance of ferreting?

'What about Dermid?' she asked. 'Are you going to do anything for him?'

'That's what I wanted to talk to you about, only we were sidetracked on to other things and then you ran away,' he said. 'I've been thinking about it, but before I can come to any decision Martha will have to meet certain conditions. I have to know what else it is that she wants.' He spoke slowly, as if thinking out loud, and Sandy took advantage of the pause to rush in impulsively with a suggestion.

'I don't think you'll have to wait until the end of the summer,' she said. 'I think if you ask Martha now . . .'

'Ask her what?' He swung round to her, obviously puzzled, and they stopped walking. Behind him she could see the bulk of Duncreggan House nestling among its trees. Moonlight shimmered on the slates of its roof, and several small moons glittered back in reflection from the dark glass of its windows.

'To marry you.' She blurted it out. 'If you and she married it would solve everything, wouldn't it? You could adopt Dermid then and bring him up as your own son.'

He was facing the moon and his face was clearly illuminated, a finely-chiselled carving in pale stone, and like stone it was devoid of expression.

'You're sure that's what Martha wants?' he asked.

'She hasn't said so in as many words, but one day when we were on the beach she told me that she would like to be married again and said she thought she'd found someone to take Crawford's place. She was drawing in the sand with a stick at the time and she drew the letter L.'

'And you put two and two together,' he mocked gently.

'Yes.'

He made no comment, but she thought his eyes glinted ironically before he turned away to walk on down the pathway to the house. She followed him and soon they were skirting the farm buildings and going round to the front steps. Light glimmered faintly through the long windows facing the driveway, and the lanterns on either side of the front door showed their usual dim yellow light and were no compensation for the lack of moonlight on this side of the house.

Sandy began to go up the steps to the door.

'Sandy, wait a minute,' said Lymond behind her, and, thinking that he had something further to say about Martha, she turned back to stand before him, looking up expectantly.

'Sandy is usually a boy's name in Scotland, short for Alexander,' he said. 'It seems odd for a girl.'

'In my case, it's short for Alexandra,' she replied.

'That makes me think of someone poised and regal.'

'Like Queen Alexandra,' she said with a laugh. 'I know, and you think I'm anything but poised and regal.'

'Quite right. I think you're leggy and coltish, not sure what you are yet,' he teased.

'Thank you. You've already made your opinion of me clear tonight. A sexless object, I think you said,' she retorted, and felt an odd urge to linger with him out there in the soft night because in the give and take of taunts there was a closeness and understanding between them which she had never experienced with anyone else.

'It'll have to be Sandy, then,' he decided. 'And now I think about it, perhaps it is suitable, for your hair is the colour of sand, not the dark ribbed stuff, but the fine silky yellow kind.'

He raised a hand and touched her hair where it lay smooth and faintly luminous against her temple. She caught her breath as a strange sensation swept through her, making her legs shake so that she couldn't have moved even if she had wanted to.

But she didn't want to. She wanted to stay there and find out what would happen next. His hand slid down the side of her face until it cupped her chin and still she didn't try to break away. There was a tense moment of waiting as if he was expecting her to pull away from him. It lasted about two heartbeats, then he bent his head and kissed her.

She offered no resistance, and when, after the first touch, his mouth opened on hers, she followed his experienced demonstration in how to kiss. Then his arms came around her and hers went up to hold him close, and for a few brief minutes both of them were too engrossed in the ancient art of lovemaking to notice what was going on about them.

Lymond broke the kiss first, still holding her closely.

'Not bad for a sexless object,' he jeered softly. 'I might make a woman of you yet.'

He kissed her again, his mouth hard and cool, and as she responded Sandy felt as if the door to a secret inner part of her was being unlocked for the first time as she was swept by an overwhelming desire to give, to hold back nothing, to let him do what he wanted with her because it was what she wanted too.

There was noise and light. A car was approaching the house from the driveway. The white glare of its headlights was all about them, harsh and cruel, no substitute for moonlight. Lymond let go of her with a softly muttered curse. The car stopped, the headlights were snapped off, the engine ceased to growl and a door opened. Sandy, hoping that Martha wasn't in the car, being brought home by the Lindsays, began to go up the steps.

'Lymond? Is that you?' The voice was female, high-pitched, a little stiff and stilted as if the owner of it was not sure how she would be received.

'Who else could it be, Helen Lindsay?' he taunted. 'I wondered when you'd find an excuse to come here.'

About to turn the knob of the front door, Sandy flinched a little, as she was sure the other woman must be flinching at the calculated cruelty of Lymond's remarks.

'There's been an accident.' Helen made the announcement breathlessly.

'Accident?' Sandy heard herself repeating, and she turned to go back down the steps, her thoughts going immediately to Martha, who should have been brought back in that car.

'Come on, Helen, stop being so damned cagey. What sort of an accident?' demanded Lymond curtly.

'Martha fell this evening at Brookfield. She broke her right leg. It was one of those silly accidents—her heel caught in a rug which skidded on the polished floor of the hall. Bill asked me to come over and tell you,' said Helen, keeping her glance steadily on Lymond, refusing to acknowledge that there was anyone else present.

'Well, she certainly couldn't have chosen a better place to break a leg, could she?' remarked Lymond with a touch of humour. 'In the house of an orthopaedic surgeon. I suppose Bill has everything under control and she's now in hospital receiving the correct treatment.'

'Oh, poor Martha!' exclaimed Sandy, thinking of Martha's pain and frustration. 'Is it a bad break?'

Helen turned to her at last. There was a little silence. Then, realising that the woman had forgotten who she was, Sandy explained.

'I'm Martha's cousin, Sandy Phillips. Naturally I'm concerned about her. Do you think I'll be able to visit her in the hospital?'

'Oh, of course. You're the little boy's nursemaid. Martha has told me about you.' There was just the suspicion of a sneer in the high-pitched voice. 'I'm afraid I couldn't tell you about the break, because the X-rays hadn't been done when I left the hospital. You'll have to find out for yourself about visiting hours.'

She turned back to Lymond, her attitude one of dismissal. Obviously she had no time for a nursemaid who allowed herself to be seen in a close amorous embrace with Caldwell of Duncreggan.

'Lymond, now that I'm here, I'd like to talk to you,' she said.

'It's late, Helen. I have to be up early in the morning,' he parried easily, and Sandy recognised only too well the signs of withdrawal in him.

'Please, Lymond.' Now there was a change. The stiffness had gone from Helen's voice. She was no longer supercilious. Her tone was low and appealing. 'It's been such a long time since we met last. I've thought of you often. I've

102

wanted many times to tell you how mistaken I was, what a fool I was. You see, I believed Crawford when he told me ...'

'Helen, this is neither the time nor the place for this sort of discussion.' Lymond's voice was rough.

'But Bill says that ...' Helen broke off, sent a glance in Sandy's direction, and remembering the moment in the pub when she had seen Helen with her guard down Sandy guessed this was another similar moment and that it wouldn't be kind or fair to stay and listen to what the woman had to say to Lymond.

'Goodnight,' she said clearly, and went up the steps, leaving behind her a rather strained silence.

She entered the house and closed the door behind her. She went slowly up the stairs, aware of a new strange heaviness of heart because those moments of moon-madness she had shared with Lymond were over, cut short by the arrival of Helen. While she had been in his arms responding to his caresses she had had a glimpse of a rare joy. If only Helen hadn't come ...

Sandy shivered a little, not with cold or fear but with a sense of frustration, of thwarted anticipation, and hurried along the passage to her room. There was no use spending time in vain regrets, she knew that, but if Helen hadn't come she and Lymond might have learned so much more about each other.

Once in bed she channelled her thoughts carefully in the direction of Martha. How long would it take to heal a broken leg? Six weeks was a period of time which suggested itself to her, but she had a feeling it depended on which part of the leg had been broken, and even if Martha was allowed out of hospital to hobble about on crutches, someone would have to look after Dermid until she had recovered.

Perhaps Martha would let her take the boy back to

Hampshire with her when she left Duncreggan next Wednesday, the day Lymond's invitation to her, to stay for two weeks, expired. She would make the suggestion to her cousin tomorrow when she visited her.

One the other hand it was possible that Lymond would decide whether Dermid should stay on at Duncreggan until his mother's leg was healed. And that depended entirely on how Lymond had received the news that Martha wanted to marry him. He had seemed surprised when told, yet Sandy was convinced that he was secretly attracted to her cousin.

What other reason could there be for his appearance in the pub at Creggan? And why had he sought her out at the dance to ask her questions about Martha's friendship with Bill Lindsay? Because, as Johnnie had hinted, Bill Lindsay presented competition. And, knowing Martha as she did, Sandy wouldn't put it past her cousin to have deliberately planned the whole thing in order to provoke a reaction in the hitherto aloof Lymond.

Anything else which had happened had been the result of the moonlight and had meant nothing, nothing at all. To kiss a girl goodnight after walking her home from a dance was probably second nature to Lymond, something he had always done as part of the fun he expected from a village dance. If it hadn't been her, it might have been the blonde barmaid, and at least it had proved to her that there was a warm and feeling man within the armour.

Moon magic, that was all it had been, and she mustn't let it mean anything more, so closing her eyes tightly she willed herself to sleep before the black knight of Duncreggan could take over and destroy her peace of mind for ever.

CHAPTER FIVE

As soon as she heard Dermid moving about and singing to himself next morning Sandy went to him and told him what had happened to his mother. He took the news quietly, thrust his hand into hers and whispered,

'You'll look after me now, won't you, Sandy?'

Touched by his trust in her, she took him downstairs to the kitchen, where as usual Nan was bustling about the cooker.

'Lymond has phoned the hospital to ask about Martha,' Nan said as she helped Sandy to porridge. That was a good sign, thought Sandy. It showed he was interested in Martha's welfare even though he always gave the impression that he wasn't.

'How is she?' she asked as she tied Dermid's bib round his neck.

'She's as comfortable as can be expected and you can go and see her this afternoon. Lymond says he'll drive you and the bairn in himself,' replied Nan.

'I suppose that means you won't be coming sailing with Ron and me this afternoon,' said Johnnie, who had just come in and taken his usual place at the table. His dark hair was spiky, as if he hadn't had time to brush it yet that morning, and his red-rimmed eyes betrayed a late night, but his grin was as cheeky as ever.

'I would like to see Martha, and she'll be expecting me and Dermid,' she replied. 'Sorry, Johnnie, but I'm sure you'll find someone else to go with you.'

'Och, I daresay we will,' he said, with a knowledgeable twinkle in his eyes.' Did you have a nice walk home in the moonlight with Lymond? Ron was a bit put out when he discovered you'd left the dance without telling him.'

'But I didn't intend to leave. I went out for a breath of

fresh air, it was so hot in there. When I came back you'd both gone. I guessed Ron had found another partner.'

'Och, no, not anyone special anyway. She was Sheila Grant who is back home for a wee holiday. She invited us to go to her home, which is in Kirkton. You were invited too, but we assumed you had better things to do.' Again his eyes twinkled knowledgeably as he noticed the colour rise slowly in her cheeks. 'You'll be staying on a bit longer with Martha laid up, won't you?' he added curiously.

'I don't know. It depends on whether I'm invited to stay,' she replied with a touch of stiffness.

'Who's going to look after Dermid if you don't?'

'Your mother could.'

'I doubt it. She's going away on Monday to stay for a while with her sister who has a small hotel in Scarborough. It's been arranged for months. Lymond has even arranged for Will Brodie's wife to come in the mornings and clean up and prepare the dinner, but she can't stay overnight to look after your cousin's child.'

'Then perhaps I'll take Dermid with me when I return to Hampshire.'

'Och, now, that would be a shame, so it would, to take the wee laddie away when he's just getting used to the place,' said Nan, coming to the table with Johnnie's breakfast. 'The bairn's home is here now, where his father grew up, and I'm sure Lymond will be asking you to stay and help out.'

But Sandy wasn't so sure, and grew even less sure on the way to the hospital that afternoon, for Lymond was as cool and aloof as ever, behaving as·if nothing at all had happened between them the previous night.

Perhaps nothing had happened, thought Sandy, as she gazed out at the rolling green countryside. Perhaps it had all been a fantasy; that recurring fantasy she experienced in which she met the black knight who rescued her from small dangers and mishaps. She gave her head a sharp

106

shake and answered one of Dermid's persistent questions. Fantasy or not, she must follow Lymond's lead, behave as if nothing had happened and remember that she was there to help her cousin achieve two aims: the financing of Dermid's education and her marriage to Lymond.

The grey granite houses of Kirkton twinkled in the sunlight, and the main street was busy with holidaymakers shopping for the weekend. Lymond found a place to park, and after telling her brusquely to wait in the car, went off down the street. He returned about five minutes later carrying a bunch of red roses, a basket of grapes and a box of chocolates. Another good sign, thought Sandy, as he gave them to her to hold, then she wondered why it gave her so little pleasure to realise that at last Lymond was responding to Martha's attempts to attract him.

The hospital was on the outskirts of the town and, although small, was shining with cleanliness inside. Even with her right leg abulge with plaster and held up in traction Martha managed to look remarkably beautiful, the pallor brought on by shock and pain making her oval face look as if it had been carved from alabaster. In contrast, her fiery hair looked brighter than ever.

She made no attempt to hide her gladness at seeing them, holding out her arms to Dermid till Sandy lifted him up to be hugged and kissed. Then it was Sandy's turn to bend down and kiss her cousin, who turned afterwards to Lymond and held out her arms to him. After a slight hesitation he moved forward, bent his dark head and kissed her on the cheek. As he straightened up he presented her with the red roses which he had been hiding behind his back.

'Oh, how gorgeous they are!' exclaimed Martha. She smelt them and gave him a glistening look. 'How did you know I just adore red roses, Lymond? Thank you very much. Sandy, will you take them and see if you can find a vase for them?'

Sandy presented the grapes and Dermid the chocolates,

then she went off to the ward office to find a vase. When she returned to the bedside Lymond was sitting in a chair, holding Dermid on his knee, and Martha was chattering away to him. It was quite a domestic little scene, thought Sandy, as she took a chair on the opposite side of the bed. Anyone coming in who didn't know would have guessed that father and child were visiting mother.

'It's almost worth breaking a leg to receive all this attention,' said Martha, turning her head to look at Sandy. 'Wasn't it a silly thing to do?'

'How bad is it?' asked Sandy.

'It's above the knee, which is why it's being held up. Bill says he'd like me to stay in here for about ten days to two weeks.' Martha looked back at Lymond. 'I'm awfully sorry,' she whispered.

'I'm afraid it'll mean Sandy will have to stay longer to look after Dermid for me.'

Sandy couldn't help but notice the sardonic twist to Lymond's mouth, the narrowing of his dark eyes. He looked as if he believed Martha had deliberately broken her leg in order to make it possible for Sandy to stay on longer at Duncreggan. And she couldn't have him thinking that, so she said hurriedly,

'I could take him to Hampshire with me when I leave on Wednesday.'

There was a short uncomfortable silence. Martha frowned at Sandy, while Lymond seemed to be deep in thought as he thrust his hands into his trouser pockets, tilted his chair on to its back legs and looked at nobody.

'Don't want you to go,' piped up Dermid suddenly, coming round the bed and plonking himself down hard in Sandy's lap as if by doing so he could prevent her from leaving and returning to Hampshire. 'Want you to stay here and look after me. Don't want to go to Hampshire. Want to stay here and go to the beach every day and play with Euan and Lorna!'

His small voice died away. He glared defiantly across the bed at Lymond, who returned the glare coolly although the corner of his mouth twitched.

'Obviously he's made his mind up,' he remarked. His glance lifted to Sandy. His dark eyes were empty of expression. 'It's up to you, now,' he said. 'Is it possible for you to stay on at Duncreggan and look after him until Martha has recovered?'

Sandy glanced at Martha, whose amber eyes had rounded appealingly.

'Please, Sandy, say you'll stay,' she pleaded. 'I'll get better faster if I know that Dermid is near by and you are looking after him.'

How could she resist an appeal like that? Even if Lymond disapproved she had to agree to stay.

'Yes, I could stay,' she said.

'Any conditions?' The jibe was quietly spoken and it made her look at him again. There was a glint of devilment in his eyes and the sight of it made her pulse quicken.

'Only one,' she retorted.

'What is it?' he asked.

'I'll stay if you'll let me do some digging either behind the castle or on the hill to see if I can find some relics which might prove there was once a sixth-century fort at Duncreggan.'

They stared at each other across the white hospital bed. For all the notice they took of them, Martha and Dermid might not have been there.

'You can dig if you want to,' he said, his voice as cool as ever. 'But not deeply and not where there is any cultivation. Provided you look after Dermid and help in the house while Nan is away.'

'Is Nan going away?' exclaimed Martha. 'I didn't know. When will she be back?'

'I'm not sure,' replied Lymond. 'She's going to stay with

her sister for a few weeks with the intention of going into partnership in the hotel business.'

'But if she goes, who will keep house at Duncreggan?' asked Martha, looking worried.

'That, my dear sister-in-law, has not yet been decided,' drawled Lymond, rising slowly to his feet. 'Meanwhile Mrs Brodie will work part-time. I've some business to attend to in the town, so I'll leave you two to catch up on the gossip. I'll be back in about half an hour and I'll see you at the main entrance, Sandy.' He turned to give Martha a long considering glance and added softly, 'Take care of yourself and do exactly what the surgeon orders—he knows best. Goodbye for now.'

He left the ward, and Martha turned her head to look at Sandy, her eyes wide with puzzlement.

'Well, what's come over him?' she said. 'He was quite charming. In fact for a while I could have imagined it was Crawford who was sitting there. Have you an explanation for such a change?'

'It could be because I told him what it is you want,' muttered Sandy, who herself a little bemused by Lymond's attitude to her cousin.

'What do you mean?' asked Martha. She raised a hand to her head. 'I'm afraid after that fall I'm not quite with it. I banged the back of my head too and Bill says I've slight concussion. Oh, Sandy, Bill's been so nice. I'm beginning to think my fall might have been a blessing in disguise, what with Lymond bringing me those gorgeous roses and with Bill being so attentive and kind.' She broke off, her eyelashes drooped over her eyes and the faintest of smiles played around her mouth. 'What did you tell Lymond I wanted?' she asked.

'You remember he asked whether I was sure that the financing of Dermid's education is all you want?' said Sandy.

'Yes, I remember.'

'And when I told you what he'd said, you said that it isn't all you want, but that you couldn't tell me exactly what it is because you're afraid it won't happen if you do,' continued Sandy slowly, because it all seemed very complicated to explain. 'Well, I guessed what it is you want. You want to marry again, so I told Lymond that.'

'And what was his reaction?' exclaimed Martha, looking suddenly disturbed.

'I'm not sure, because he didn't say anything, but I think it might account for the change in his attitude today. I believe he's really attracted to you, Martha, only he's been hiding his feelings because you've been widowed only recently and also because he's not been sure about your feelings towards him.'

Martha stared at her, then laughed rather strangely.

'I suppose you could be right,' she said, and Sandy glanced at her uneasily.

'I hope you don't mind me telling him. You see, I thought at the time I wouldn't be here for much longer and that it might urge him to come to some decision and help all three of you in the long run, you, him and Dermid,' she explained earnestly.

'Yes, it might help in the long run,' murmured Martha enigmatically, a slight frown marring the usual smoothness of her forehead.

'Are you feeling tired?' asked Sandy anxiously. She was more than a little puzzled by her cousin's lethargic behaviour. She had expected Martha to be triumphant as a result of learning that at last a chink had been found in Lymond's armour and that there was a warm human being capable of normal emotions hiding behind his customary cool, indifferent and sometimes dour behaviour.

'A little,' sighed Martha. 'Bill said I'll feel very tired for a while because of the shock and the pain. Did Helen bring you the news about me?'

'Yes. We'd just got back from the village dance.'

'Who's we?' asked Martha, her interest reviving as she sensed an amatory adventure.

'Lymond and I.' Sandy did her best to control the rise of colour to her face as she recalled the circumstances of Helen's arrival at Duncreggan the previous evening. Not for the first time in her life she wished she didn't have a thin fair skin which flushed easily.

'The last time I saw him he was doing a good line with the blonde barmaid in the pub,' said Martha drily. 'I remember thinking at the time he had something in common with Crawford besides looks, after all. So he changed partners when he got to the dance, did he?'

'Yes, he did,' said Sandy rather faintly. 'But it was only to ask me about you. He'd seen you with the Lindsays and he wanted to know how you'd managed to become friendly with them.'

Resentment flashed in Martha's eyes.

'Oh, I do hope he isn't going to be difficult just because of that old feud. I hope he doesn't think he has a right to choose my friends,' she said sharply.

'No, no, it wasn't that,' explained Sandy hurriedly. 'He's surprised because you've found friends in that quarter, he said. Apparently, some years ago, Helen's mother discouraged a friendship which was developing between Helen and Crawford. You know, Martha, that could be the reason why she snubbed you when she first met you and made all those other odd remarks.'

'You mean she was suffering from jealousy because I had managed to marry Crawford and she hadn't?' queried Martha.

'That's right.'

'An interesting point of view, little cousin, but for once I think you're wrong. Helen is jealous of me, but not for that reason,' replied Martha, smiling. Then her face changed and she exclaimed, 'Oh, Sandy, quick! Take the chocolates

112

from Dermid before he's sick. Dermid love, they aren't for you but for me.'

Dermid didn't take kindly to having the chocolates removed from his grasp, and roared his objection, with the result that Sandy had to bid Martha a hasty goodbye and hurry the child off to a washroom to clean him up before going to the main entrance to meet Lymond.

He wasn't there—which wasn't surprising because the half hour wasn't up—so, since the afternoon sun was warm and mellow, Sandy took Dermid to a small park nearby where he was able to swing and seesaw for a while.

It was as they were returning slowly to the hospital that Sandy saw Lymond walking along the road. He was walking slowly too and he was not alone. Beside him walked a tall woman whose brown hair had a reddish tinge in the bright sunlight. She was Helen Lindsay.

So that was the business he had had to attend to in the town, thought Sandy, and she began to wonder if the arrangement to meet had been made the previous night.

'Am I late?' Lymond's voice was amused and startled her. She turned to find him beside her. He had come up while she had been busy with her imaginings about him and Helen Lindsay. She glanced quickly behind him and then around, not bothering to hide the fact that she was looking for his recent companion.

'Helen has gone into the hospital,' he explained coolly, almost as if answering a question she had asked. 'She's working there this weekend, taking the place of a doctor who is on holiday. She's doing locum work until she can set up in practice here. What would you like to do now?'

'Do?' She blinked up at him, surprised that he should ask her such a question. The arrogant Lymond Caldwell she had known until that point of time never asked other people what they wanted to do. He assumed usually that they would do what he wanted.

'The rest of the afternoon is ours,' he said. 'We have

113

Dermid with us, so you don't have to worry about getting back to Duncreggan to look after him. I've nothing pressing to do there, either, as it happens. Perhaps you'd like to do some shopping?'

He was making an effort to be pleasant, she was sure, for he wasn't the sort of man who would like trailing around shops after a woman. Glancing sideways at him, she tried to evaluate his mood. As usual his face gave no hint of what he was feeling or thinking, so she took a chance.

'Do you think we could go to see the Mote?' she asked.

'The what?'

'The Mote. It's an earthwork a few miles away from here. Your father mentions it in his history. It was an important place when this part of the country was an independent Celtic kingdom. You might be interested in it, being a councillor, because it was a place where the local kings held councils and made laws. I'd like to see it because it's one of the most interesting historical sites around here.'

He looked down at her, his eyes narrow. For a moment she thought he was going to refuse to take her to find the place, and she began to search her mind for further arguments to persuade him. Then he smiled and her heart did an odd little flutter, which she quelled at once.

'I should have known that shops wouldn't interest you,' he drawled. 'All right, we'll go and find this Mote you've read about, and then you'll never be able to accuse me again of not taking an interest in the past.'

The way to the Mote was along a narrow country lane which turned off the main road to Dumfries. It twisted between humpy green fields and occasionally dipped down to run close to the course of a shallow river, the waters of which gleamed gold and green between grassy willow-edged banks.

Sandy sat forward in her seat, eagerly scanning the scenery ahead and watching for a mound of earth which would mark the site of the Mote. When it appeared, rising up out of a field, she was surprised to see it was much higher than she had expected, about seventy feet high with sloping sides and a flat summit.

'There it is,' she exclaimed. 'Over to the right.'

'We should be able to park quite close to it. Nothing much comes along this road,' said Lymond.

The place was in fact deserted, and as she stepped through the gap in the dry stone wall which edged the field, Sandy experienced that familiar feeling of stepping back in time. The smell of wild grasses and flowers, the sweet shrill of the meadow lark singing in the clear air, the tinkle of the river, the absence of all noise of traffic enhanced the feeling. She stared up at the mound of earth which had once been a court of justice, and for a moment imagined it thronged with people come to watch and hear the trials of capital offenders.

'Come on, continue with the history lesson,' teased Lymond making her jump and bringing her back to reality. 'I'm really very ignorant and had no idea this place existed. What does it represent?'

'It's a very remarkable example of a fort. The central mound with the flat top would be the main part of the citadel. Around it is the base court which has an extended platform. Below are the ditches dug to protect it from attack. It must have taken a long time to build, or there must have been many willing hands to do it.'

'But there's nothing like this at Duncreggan,' he said.

'Not obviously, yet not only your father but also an earlier local surveyor believed that there was, and your father actually found artefacts. Didn't he ever tell you of his finds?'

He slanted a sardonic glance.

'No, he didn't. His digging in the past happened after I left home nearly twelve years ago. Communication between us was never at a high level, and when I returned about two and a half years ago he was too paralysed by a stroke to speak properly. What did he find?'

'A brooch and some moulds.'

'And you want to dig in the hopes of finding more?'

'Yes, I do, and Ron Carson is going to find out if his father has any of the aerial photographs of the area which he commissioned at one time. They would show if there were any shapes of previous settlement under the present surface of the land.'

'I see.' He glanced away to the mound which towered above them.

'It would help enormously if I could find the brooch and the moulds which your father dug up,' she went on. 'I suppose you've no idea where they might be?'

'Look in the library. They're bound to be there.'

Sandy became aware suddenly that while they had been talking Dermid had wandered away. She glanced round and saw him trotting through the long waving grasses towards the river.

'Dermid, be careful,' she called. 'I'll have to go after him,' she flung over her shoulder at Lymond, and darted after the little boy.

As she approached the bank of the river she heard the steady roar of water pouring over a ledge and could actually see the cascade of white foam as it fell several feet into a pool. Dermid, in his eagerness to see more of the waterfall, tripped over the exposed root of a willow tree and fell into the pool.

It wasn't very deep, but at that point the water swirled and bubbled as a result of its steep fall, creating a current against which the howling, floundering little boy had no resistance. It caught his light body and swept him on downriver.

'Sandy!' he shrieked, and without hesitation, without even removing her shoes, she waded straight into the river, and gasped with surprise when the water in the pool rose as high as her waist.

116

Moving as fast as she could, she started off downstream, calling to Dermid that she was coming. She could see him desperately trying to do the dog paddle she had taught him, and within seconds she had reached him and was holding him, a wet sobbing bundle who clutched her round the neck.

Looking round, she found that the river, although considerably shallower at this point, was much wider. She started to make for the nearest bank when her foot slipped on a wet stone and she lost her balance and sat down abruptly in the water. Dermid, disconcerted by this new accident, yelled louder, but as Sandy tried to get up she slipped again and sat down, realising that the encumbrance of the child was making it difficult for her to rise.

'Hold tight, Dermid,' she comforted him. 'This time we're going to make it.'

And they did, because someone was there helping her up and there was an arm round her shoulders holding her steady.

'You looked as if you needed some help,' said Lymond from behind her. 'Let me take the lad.'

She turned carefully and to her surprise Dermid went to his uncle willingly, winding his little arms closely round Lymond's neck as if he found comfort in the broad shoulders which supported him, and, because he was stronger and could hold the boy with one arm, Lymond was able to balance better. He was soon depositing Dermid on the bank and turning back to give Sandy a helping hand.

What a mess she must look, thought Sandy, as she took off her shoes and emptied water out of them. Her dress was soaked and even her hair was partially wet. Once again Lymond had had to come to her rescue, and yet in contrast to herself he had managed to preserve his usual casual elegance because he had had the forethought to remove his jacket, his shoes and socks and had rolled up his trousers before wading into the river.

Now he had Dermid on his knee and was talking gently while he removed the child's wet shirt and shorts. Dermid was sitting quietly watching his uncle with big golden eyes while he chewed the end of a finger.

'Now that we've got rid of those soggy things we'll have to find something for you to wear to keep you warm,' said Lymond. With a quick smooth action he pulled his black polo-necked jersey over his head. 'You can have this because I have a jacket to wear. It's a bit big, but it's better than nothing.' He slanted a glance at Sandy. 'I'm afraid I've nothing for you.'

'Oh, that's all right. I'll be fine,' she replied quickly. She was aware suddenly of his maleness, of the smooth shift of taut muscle under bare ivory-tinted skin, of the rough criss-cross of black hairs on a broad chest, of the lean flatness below the bulge of the rib cage. 'Thank you for rescuing me again,' she added.

'It was you who were doing the rescuing,' he replied. 'Lucky for Dermid you can move so fast.' Again he glanced at her, took in her damp-darkened hair, the clinging wetness of her dress, the length of her bare wet legs. 'You remind me a little of someone I used to know.'

'Who?' she asked.

'My mother,' was the unexpected reply. 'I don't mean I see you as a mother figure or even that you look like her,' he was quick to add as he noticed her glance of surprise. 'But you react in a similar way to situations, impulsively, without thought for yourself. And then you have this enthusiasm for history. She was enthusiastic about sailing, and in a way her enthusiasm led to her being drowned.'

'I didn't realise you remembered her.'

'Crawford and I were ten, nearly eleven, when she was drowned, so I remember her well,' he replied coolly. He pushed Dermid off his knees and stood up, then lifted the little boy, who looked rather pathetic in the over-long, over-wide sweater, and held him against his shoulder. 'I

118

left my shoes and jacket higher up the bank. We'll collect them and then go home. This lad has had enough excitement for one day.'

Dermid sat quietly on Sandy's knee on the drive back to Duncreggan, and she was silent too, half day-dreaming, her mind filled with errant thoughts about the Mote, about Lymond's mother Phillida, who had suddenly ceased to be a frail wayward ghost and took on substance as a woman who lived enthusiastically and had died while pursuing that enthusiasm. She thought too about Helen Lindsay and then about Martha, and bestirred herself to tell Lymond that her cousin had liked his roses very much. But since he only grunted in reply she didn't say any more, recognising that he had withdrawn again, and then wondering why he had bothered to take her to the Mote. Considering what had happened he wouldn't be in a hurry to go anywhere with her again, she thought with a rueful grin. From now on he would probably steer clear of her and her tendency to fall over.

She was surprised by a feeling of gladness when they reached the lichen-covered gateposts; a sense of having returned home as they went up the rutted driveway. The house of pale stone looked gracious and welcoming, and there was a homeliness about the untidy, gaudily painted kitchen which was comforting.

Nan fussed over them, insisting on taking Dermid upstairs herself to bath him while Sandy changed into dry clothes. As they ate the meal she had prepared they told her about Martha and about the Mote. When the meal was over Sandy took Dermid up to bed, where he fell asleep almost at once.

Back in the kitchen she had another cup of tea with Nan. Lymond had gone out again and Johnnie was still down at Creggan.

'Lymond told me that you might stay in Scarborough and go into the hotel business with your sister,' said Sandy.

'Aye. She's been wanting me to do it for years, but couldn't leave Gavin,' replied Nan. 'Now there's nothing to keep me here. Johnnie is old enough to take care of himself, and I'm thinking Lymond will be wanting to marry soon.'

'Oh, really. Has he anyone in mind?' asked Sandy.

'There's no telling with him. Close he is, like his father was. He's never been one for sharing his secrets with anyone. But I can't see him living here for long without a woman to keep him company. Quiet he may be, but he's a Caldwell and the blood runs hot in his veins.'

Sandy was silent, remembering Martha's suggestion that Nan had been more than a housekeeper to Gavin Caldwell. Being a great respecter of other people's privacy she would never even hint to the older woman about the story that she had been the old man's mistress during the years she had kept house for him, but Nan was also a Caldwell and wasn't it possible that the blood had run hot in her veins, too, at one time?

'Lymond was telling me this afternoon that his mother was very keen on sailing,' she commented, thinking she might get Nan to talk about Phillida.

'Aye, she was a live-wire, was Phillida, always on the go. Gavin encouraged her to sail, even bought her a boat. Of course there was a lot of gossip, for she was down at the yacht club by the hour in the summer, and people who had nothing better to do used to talk about her and the men she met there. But she didn't care what people said. That was the trouble. And she was impulsive, never thinking of herself, so that when Stewart Lindsay bought a new boat and wanted to try it out, who offered to go with him on that terrible windy day but Phillida, and unfortunately no one else.'

'Stewart Lindsay?' said Sandy. 'Was he any relation to Bill Lindsay?'

'Aye, his father, so you can imagine the scandal when their bodies were washed up further down the Firth, the

120

sly suggestions that were made that they were running away together. It broke Gavin's heart.'

Nan's face was dark and morose as she swirled the dregs of tea in Sandy's cup and emptied them into a slop bowl on the table. She began to twist the cup this way and that as she peered at the arrangement of tealeaves in the bottom of it.

'Was there any truth in the suggestions?' asked Sandy.

'Who's to say? Knowing Phillida I don't think there was. But only she and Stewart knew the truth and they didn't survive,' sighed Nan, gazing into the cup again. 'So you'll be staying on here a wee while, yet, to look after Dermid?'

'Yes,' replied Sandy. 'What can you see in the cup?'

'Och, I can see a dark handsome man in your life,' said Nan, and a smile chased fleetingly across her face. 'But that wouldn't be unusual while you stay in this house. And then I see a woman, not your cousin, a tall woman . . .'

'Helen Lindsay,' said Sandy, the name leaping into her mind for no apparent reason.

'Now whatever made you think of her?' demanded Nan, looking up at her in surprise.

'She was at the hospital this afternoon. I saw her talking to Lymond. Do you know her?'

'Aye, I do that,' said Nan flatly, placing the cup back in its saucer. 'When she was a girl she was forever coming here after the twins, to play with them. And after Phillida was drowned her parents tried to keep her from coming, but she always found a way to meet them somewhere. When she was older and here only for the holidays like them, she'd come asking me where she could find them, as if I knew where they'd gone gallivanting. I used to ask them where they were going and all they used to say was "Out". Och, wild as hawks they were, and no one safe from their mischievous ways. I'd heard Helen was back and wasn't surprised when Lymond told me it was she who brought the news about your cousin. She'll be here again. It's there in

121

your fortune. And you'll take care, when she comes, because she's not above causing trouble.'

Sunday came and went and on Monday morning Nan departed, taken to Dumfries by Johnnie to catch a train which would take her to Carlisle. From there another train would take her across the country to the east coast. Mrs Brodie arrived to do the washing, cooking and cleaning, so that Sandy still had all morning free to attend to Dermid.

While he rested in the afternoon she went behind the castle where the ground was rough, but although the soil was fairly loose it was covered by bracken, small whin-bushes and brambles which made penetration difficult. Looking round, assessing the land, she decided that the only place where she might find anything of interest would be on the hill behind the house.

Returning to the house, she went up for Dermid and they went to collect eggs, after which they walked down to the beach as usual to play with Euan and Lorna. When she went back to Duncreggan she prepared high tea, and after the meal was over Johnnie drove her in Lymond's car into Kirkton to visit Martha.

Several days passed in similar fashion. Nothing unusual happened. She tried digging on the hill, but with little success, and in the end decided to wait until Ron Carson brought her the photographs. From past experience she knew that they would prove once and for all if there were any signs of early settlement and whether excavation was worthwhile.

One afternoon when rain blotted out the landscape with a fine grey mist which made working out of doors a wet business, Sandy decided to search the library for the brooch and the clay moulds that Gavin Caldwell had found. The room looked gloomier than ever when she entered it, and she stood for a while looking round, wondering where to start her search.

122

Her glance lingered on the books. Thinking how forlorn and neglected they looked in their undusted, mildewed state, she recalled her offer to tidy them so that someone could come and appraise their worth. On sudden impulse she went to the kitchen and into the big closet where Nan stored all the house-cleaning equipment, and where she was sure she had seen a step-ladder. It was still there, and although it was rather dilapidated, it seemed steady enough. She lugged it through to the library and went back for a duster.

She started with the top shelf on the left-hand side of the fireplace. She took each book out, dusted it and placed it on the top step of the ladder, intending to clear the shelf so that she could dust it before returning the books.

Many of the books concerned military history and she spent some time leafing through them. She was engrossed in reading a passage in one of them when Lymond spoke to her from the doorway. His voice startled her and she dropped the book, which fell with a thud to the floor.

'What did you say?' she asked as he came across the room to pick up the book and hand it to her. Since their outing to the Mote he had kept very much to himself, as she had guessed he would, and apart from mealtimes she had seen very little of him.

He was dressed in the denim trousers and denim shirt which he usually wore for working on the farm and he was wearing the heavy rubber boots which were necessary at all times for walking about the fields. If Nan were here, thought Sandy inconsequently, she would have told him to remove his boots before stepping out of the kitchen.

'I asked you if the ladder is safe,' he said.

'I think so. But I'm not making much progress. I'm still on the first shelf. The trouble is they're all so interesting.'

'Have you given up digging?'

'No, but I think it would be wise to wait until I can have a look at an aerial photograph. I'm hoping Ron will bring

123

one tonight. I came in here to look for the artefacts and then remembered I'd said I'd tidy the books for you.'

'You don't have to,' he murmured.

'I'd like to,' she replied, feeling suddenly and overwhelmingly shy of him, so she turned away to take down another book and dust it.

'What's the latest news on Martha?' he asked.

'Oh, she's getting better, but Bill won't let her up yet. He says he might let her leave hospital at the end of next week. It all depends on how she gets on with the crutches, and also what arrangements can be made for her here to have a bedroom on the ground floor. Do you think that could be managed?'

He shrugged his shoulders.

'I suppose the dining room could be made into some sort of bedroom. Better ask Johnnie to give you a hand in moving some furniture,' he replied indifferently, and reached up a hand to take one of the books off the pile. Head bent, he leafed through it, and Sandy stared down at his rough black hair thinking what a puzzle he was.

He could have asked her about Martha at any mealtime during the past week, but he hadn't and it seemed to her now that he hadn't even listened when she had ventured information about her cousin.

'She's wondering why you haven't been to visit her again,' she said abruptly, trying to put a note of censure into her voice.

'Why should I visit her again?' he countered coolly, still looking down at the book. 'You go every day, and anything she might have to say to me could be relayed to me by you. That's what you're here for, isn't it?'

The jibe didn't go unnoticed, and Sandy was strongly tempted to hit him on the top of the head with a book for being so annoying.

'Have you a message for me from her?' he asked, looking up with a glint of mockery in his eyes as if he sensed her irritation.

'I . . . I could shake you!' she retorted furiously.

'Why? What have I done?' he exclaimed, his eyes widening in mock innocence.

'It's what you haven't done. Anyone would think you have no idea how to court a woman,' she replied.

'And whom should I be courting?'

'Martha, of course. I can't do any more. I've told you what she wants. The rest is up to you. She can't do anything while she's lying in hospital with a broken leg, but you could . . .' She broke off as she realised he was watching her with eyes which were brimful of laughter.

'Go on,' he urged. 'This is proving to be most instructive. What could I do?'

'You could go and see her,' she added rather lamely.

'But you've told me she'll be back here at the end of next week, so I'll see her then,' he argued mildly, although she saw that glint of devilment in his eyes.

'I know I did, but . . .' A new thought leapt into her mind, and she realised she might have made an embarrassing mistake. 'You do want to marry Martha, don't you?' she asked anxiously.

'I'm not aware that I've ever said I want to marry anyone,' he parried.

'But you said the other night that you might have found a flower to pick which you want to keep, and Nan says she thinks you'll want to marry soon because she can't imagine you living here alone without a woman to keep you company . . .'

'And you did your usual arithmetic,' he interrupted her coldly, and she could tell by the tautening of his face that he was annoyed that his possible plans for the future had been discussed by her and Nan. 'I suppose you assumed I'd marry Martha because that fits in nice and neatly with some plan she has concocted to provide Dermid with a father and herself with a position in this community at the same time.'

He had returned the book to the pile on the ladder and had folded his arms across his chest and was now looking up at her, the expression in his eyes challenging. Sandy stared back at him in dismay. It sounded very much as if he still considered Martha to be nothing more than a hard-headed, scheming social climber.

'Then why did you give Martha the red roses?' she countered weakly.

'I'm not so lacking in courtesy that I'd visit anyone in hospital without taking some flowers. If it had been Nan or Mrs Brodie I'd have done the same,' he retorted in the same hard voice. 'Surely Martha didn't read more into that gesture than was intended?'

'I . . . I think she might have done,' she replied cautiously, realising she was on shaky ground now. 'She said, after you had gone, how different you seemed and how she could have imagined you were Crawford sitting there and talking to her.' She saw his face take on a sceptical expression and added quickly, 'I told her I thought the difference might be due to the fact that I'd told you she wants to marry.' Her voice sank to a low mortified murmur. 'I suppose you think I'm very foolish?' she added.

'And not very good at putting two and two together,' he jeered. 'Why don't you stop trying to add up? Why don't you stop trying to push us all into roles we have no wish to play? I consider marriage to be a very serious matter. A wife like Martha would be a very costly item to add to an already strained budget. She likes being petted with gifts. She would want to alter the house all at once, modernise it, and quite frankly I'm not prepared to foot the expense of such a wife.'

'Oh! There's more to marriage than . . . than footing expense,' she exploded. 'There's the love and companionship with someone you like.'

126

'Admittedly,' Lymond replied with suspicious gravity, and the tell-tale muscle twitched at the corner of his mouth so that she knew he was laughing at her. 'But it's possible to obtain both those without the bonds of matrimony. Or perhaps you didn't know.'

'Oh, I think you're the most provoking man I've ever met!' she fumed as his mockery got beneath her skin. She picked up a book to throw at him, the ladder swayed precariously and tipped over. As it went from beneath her feet Sandy seemed to hang in the air for a second. She felt arms close about her as Lymond tried to block her fall, but her weight falling against him suddenly knocked him off balance, and they both collapsed in a heap on the floor.

As once she tried to struggle up and away from him, but his arms tightened around her. He was sitting behind her and she felt the roughness of his cheek and the hardness of his jawbone against her face as he pulled her back against him to whisper in her ear.

'Rescue number five, fair damsel,' he said on a note of laughter. 'It wasn't quite as successful as the others, but it has resulted in a most interesting situation, and I think I deserve a reward for cushioning your fall.'

This suggestion, coming as it did after his most recent sardonic remark about love and companionship being available outside marriage, brought home to Sandy more than ever how he regarded her. She was someone who could be kissed and made love to for free!

'Please let me go,' she said coldly, sitting up stiffly as far away from him as possible.

'Not yet,' he teased. 'I haven't had much chance lately to continue the process of turning you into a woman.'

'And you're not getting a chance now,' she retorted furiously, trying to unclasp his hands from her waist. 'I don't want to be kissed by you.'

'I think you do,' he taunted, and she made the mistake of turning her head to look at him as she prepared to fling a retort at him. At once his hands left her waist and cupped her face. Caught and held spellbound as his mouth approached hers, Sandy heard a noise and stiffened. Lymond heard it too, for he released her and glanced towards the door. Sandy turned and looked that way too.

The door was being pushed open slowly. A head wearing a floppy-brimmed blue waterproof hat appeared first round the edge of the door. It was followed by an elegant figure which was belted into a blue trench-coat-style raincoat. Under the brim of the hat Helen Lindsay's blue eyes sparkled frostily as she stared at the two people who were sitting so close together on the floor.

CHAPTER SIX

'WHATEVER are you doing?' exclaimed Helen.

'Dusting the books,' replied Lymond coolly, getting to his feet and helping Sandy to hers. 'Sandy was on the ladder. It tipped over and she fell.' Casually he picked up the ladder and propped it against the bookshelves.

'Oh, did she?' Helen's eyebrows arched superciliously as she glanced at Sandy, who decided suddenly to pick up the books from the floor in an attempt to hide her face, which was betraying her as usual. 'I knocked on the front door, but when no one came I just walked right in. You must have been too busy to hear me.' There was just enough irony in her tone to make Sandy glance at Lymond. He seemed unperturbed, however, and was gazing at Helen with an expression of amusement on his face.

'To what do we owe this visit of yours?' he asked mockingly. 'Don't tell me there's been *another* accident.'

'No, thank goodness, and Martha, you'll be pleased to know, is making good progress. She's been moving around on crutches this morning. I looked in on her just before I left the hospital. Actually I've come to see Dermid. It's such a wet day I thought he might like to come over to Brookfield and play with Euan and Lorna. That is if you agree, Lymond?'

'Where Dermid goes for the afternoon has nothing to do with me,' he answered carelessly. 'Sandy's in charge of him, so fix it up with her. It's time I went back to work. We've erected a new barn and while the weather's wet we're finishing off the interior. Excuse me.'

'But, Lymond——' said Helen, urgently, following him out of the room into the hall. Alone, Sandy listened to the retreating sound of voices and footsteps as she piled the books which had fallen off the ladder on the floor. They would have to stay there until she could find another, safer ladder to use, she thought.

It was time to see if Dermid was awake, so she went out of the room, closing the door after her. There was no sign of Lymond or Helen in the hall. Hands to her cheeks, which were still hot, Sandy ran up the stairs, glad to have something to do so that she wouldn't be thinking of her own behaviour down there in the library when Lymond had attempted to kiss her.

Dermid was excited by the suggestion that he should go and play with Euan and Lorna, and he bounced about making washing and dressing him difficult. When he was ready Sandy took him downstairs and they met Helen who was just coming from the direction of the kitchen.

'I thought I might have a word with Nan, but she isn't in the kitchen,' she explained. 'Have you any idea where she is?'

'Didn't Lymond tell you? She's gone to Scarborough for a few weeks,' replied Sandy.

'Then who is doing the housekeeping?'

'Mrs Brodie comes every morning.'

'And in the afternoon?' Helen's eyes were frosty again

as their glance went over Sandy's shirt and jeans.

'There's just me,' replied Sandy brightly.

'You're here alone, with Lymond?' exclaimed Helen.

'Dermid and Johnnie are here too,' said Sandy coolly.

Helen made a gesture with her hand as if to indicate that neither Dermid nor Johnnie counted.

'But, my dear, is it wise?' she drawled.

'There was no alternative but for me to stay here,' replied Sandy. 'Martha wants Dermid and myself near while she's in hospital, and Lymond said we could stay.'

'I see. Well, all I can say is, don't let staying here go to your head,' snapped Helen. Then with a complete change of attitude she bent down to Dermid and said, 'Hello, darling. Are you coming with me to see Euan and Lorna? They have lots of toys you can play with and you can stay and have tea with them. Would you like that?'

'Yes, please,' smiled Dermid charmingly as he clung to Sandy's hand and swung one leg in the air. 'But only if Sandy comes too.'

'Now that's a good idea,' said Helen, much to Sandy's surprise. 'Would you like to come?' she asked, straightening up. 'My mother is having some local ladies in for afternoon tea. You could join them. It would make quite a change for you. Better than dusting old books and falling off ladders.' As she made the last remark there was a glint in her eyes which seemed to show that she hadn't believed Lymond's laconic explanation of what he and Sandy had been doing in the library.

'I'd have to ask Johnnie if he'll collect the eggs for me. It's one of Nan's jobs that I've been doing,' said Sandy.

'Well, go and do that. And change into a dress or a skirt. My grandmother is staying at Brookfield too and she's very formal. She likes women to wear skirts when they're invited to tea. She's taken a great liking to your cousin because she says Martha always looks so ladylike, and I wouldn't like you to let her down.'

Leaving Dermid with Helen in the kitchen, Sandy went to find Johnnie, who agreed to collect the eggs for her, and then she went to her room to change.

How patronising Helen was, she thought, as she changed into a pale green cotton top which had long sleeves and a scooped-out neckline. She fastened a wrap-round calf-length dark green denim skirt round her waist and began to brush her hair. How nasty Helen was, in fact. And what had she meant by those remarks about it not being wise to stay in the same house as Lymond and about not letting it go to her head? Surely the woman didn't think . . . ?

Sandy stared at her reflection. Of course, that was it. And considering the situation in which Helen had discovered her with Lymond just recently, the bad reputations where women were concerned which all the Caldwell men seemed to have had, to say nothing of the gossip about Phillida Caldwell's behaviour, Helen had every right to assume that there was something going on between Lymond and his sister-in-law's nursemaid.

Oh, how infuriating and unjust! Sandy slammed the brush down, snatched up her satchel handbag, slung it over her shoulder and marched out of the room, along the passage and down the stairs. Just because she, a single girl, was living in the same house as a Black Caldwell without the presence of any other woman, people were going to gossip.

The drive to Brookfield, down the road, past the horse-shoe bay where the sand was covered that day by grey wind-tossed water which splashed against the rocks, was made in Helen's new car.

'I got it yesterday,' announced Helen chattily. 'It's nice to feel independent again. I'm hoping by the end of the month I'll be in partnership with Dr Parker in Kirkton. When I was training to be a doctor I always hoped that one day I'd be able to practise medicine in this district where my family come from, and now at last it looks as if my wish is coming true. Have you ever been to Brookfield before?'

'No. Martha tells me it's a lovely house.'

'It is. My grandfather built it as a place to which he could retire, and we always came here for our holidays from Glasgow. He was a partner in a very successful freight business, and my father inherited the partnership from him. When my father died my mother took over his position in the company. She has always been a very determined, tough-minded business woman. Considering what happened to my father it's as well she has been.'

As soon as she stepped into Brookfield, Sandy knew why her cousin preferred it to Duncreggan House. No expense had been spared in its decoration and furnishings, and it lacked nothing in the way of modern conveniences. Shining parquet floors and pastel-shaded walls provided a background for comfortable furniture in which gleaming wood was combined with chintz upholstery. It had a sharp cleanliness and neatness about it which indicated regular cleaning and maintenance, but in contrast with the mellow gracious dustiness and untidiness of Duncreggan, it struck Sandy as lacking in warmth and friendliness.

Helen's mother, Ada Lindsay, widow of Stewart Lindsay who had been drowned with Phillida Caldwell, struck her in the same way, cold and crisp. Her greying hair was set in stiff waves, her blue eyes had a frosty glint, her pale fawn twin-set was neat and plain and the pleats of her kilt-like skirt had the sharpness of knives.

'You're not at all like Martha,' she said when Sandy was introduced to her. 'Bring the child into the lounge to meet Grandma and then he can go to the playroom.'

In contrast to her daughter-in-law, Grace Lindsay was a good-humoured old lady, long-jawed and freckle-faced like Bill, and her shrewd grey eyes had a mischievous twinkle in them as she patted Dermid's dark head and said,

'I never thought I'd see the day when Phillida Caldwell's

grandson would be welcome in this house. He's like her, don't you think, Ada?'

'I suppose there could be a likeness,' replied Ada coldly. 'I haven't had time to study him. Come along now, dear,' she said to Dermid, 'I'll take you to the playroom.'

Dermid gripped Sandy's hand hard and glared at Ada as if he sensed she was not entirely friendly towards him.

'Sandy come too,' he insisted.

'I'll come,' said Sandy quickly, to comfort him. She glanced at Ada. 'I expect he feels a little strange. He'll be all right once he's with Euan and Lorna.'

Ada's eyebrows arched in the same way that Helen's did.

'Very well,' she agreed rather reluctantly. 'But it would be a pity if he became too accustomed to being with you. After all, the day will come when you'll have to leave him to return to England, won't it? I've always been a great believer in not letting children have their own way too much; then when they grow up they can cope with separation and disappointment much better.'

Sandy would have liked to argue Dermid's case, but she held her tongue. Instinct warned her that to argue with Ada would be no good. She was relieved to find that the playroom was a bright cheerful room and that Euan and Lorna were overjoyed to see Dermid. He soon forgot his reservations about being parted from her as he was drawn into some game, and, after a few minutes of talking to Miss Dobie, the nanny, who didn't seem to be quite such a battleaxe after all, Sandy was able to go back to the lounge.

Several women had already arrived and were sitting about chatting. Helen introduced her to them and she found herself sitting beside a pleasant middle-aged woman who said,

'My daughter met you the other night at the hotel in Creggan. You were with Ron Carson. She tells me you're staying at Duncreggan House just now, minding Crawford Caldwell's little boy.'

Sandy felt that every eye had turned in her direction, even though all the other women continued to chatter to each other.

'Yes, that's right,' she said quietly.

'And how do you like living there?' One of the younger women had leaned forward to speak to her. 'I'm told it's a wee bit dilapidated, and everyone says that Nan Currie was never the best of housekeepers.'

'I like it,' replied Sandy coolly. 'It has great character and charm.'

'You could be describing its present owner, couldn't she?' said the younger woman, looking round at the others, and everyone laughed, although Helen's eyes flashed and the colour deepened in her cheeks as she glared across the room at Sandy.

'How, is Nan, these days?' asked another woman. 'She missed the last meeting of the Rural Institute.'

'She's away just now, in Scarborough. Isn't that right, Sandy?' said Helen, and this time they didn't try to hide their avid interest with chatter. They all turned to look at Sandy, some with raised eyebrows, others with scarcely concealed malice, but what struck her most was the ice-cold stare of Ada Lindsay as she raised the elegant silver teapot to pour more tea into yet another dainty china cup.

It was Grace Lindsay who came to her rescue by quite blatantly changing the subject, and there was no further discussion about Duncreggan or its owner.

But Sandy couldn't say she felt comfortable during the next hour, and she was glad when some of the women rose to take their departure and she was able to slip away to the playroom. There she found Bill Lindsay, who had just come home, having a romp with the children, and when she told him she thought it was time she took Dermid home he said,

'Never mind about Helen. I'll run you over, and Euan and Lorna can come for the ride.'

This suggestion was greeted with great glee by the children. Soon they were in the back of Bill's estate car and Sandy was saying goodbye to Ada Lindsay on the steps of the house.

'You must come again,' she said surprisingly. 'We haven't had much time to talk. Come over any time you want. It must be lonely for you over at the big house without your cousin. I've been thinking, Bill,' she added, turning to her son, 'it would be nice if we could look after Dermid while Martha is in hospital, and she could come here to stay while she's recuperating. You could keep an eye on her then, and it would free Sandy and enable her to go back to England.'

'Do you want to go back to England?' Bill asked, giving her a shrewd grey glance.

'There's no urgency. Martha knows I'll stay for as long as she needs me,' said Sandy, wondering why Ada Lindsay kept harping on the fact that she should go back to England.

'Of course, she knows that. But I'm sure she wouldn't want you to be alone at Duncreggan House while Nan is away. I expect you haven't given it a thought, Sandy, but here people are very conventional in their outlook, and any deviation from the usual code tends to cause gossip. I'll let you go now ... but do think about what I've said. Goodbye.'

Once in the car as it wound along the narrow lane which led from the house back to the road, Sandy turned to Bill.

'Do you think you could tell me why your mother and some of the other ladies are so worried about my being at Duncreggan House?' she asked.

'As far as I can tell from my mother's recent remarks, I

should say she doesn't like you virtually alone in Lymond Caldwell's house,' he replied with a grin.

'I thought that might be the case. It's very unjust of her,' observed Sandy, and he gave her a sidelong glance.

'Maybe, but unfortunately the Caldwell family, women as well as men, have had the reputation of forming what I believe are now called irregular relationships with members of the opposite sex.' Bill's voice was very dry.

'You mean like Phillida Caldwell going sailing with your father when no one else would go, and having the misfortune to be drowned with him, and Nan Currie living all those years with Gavin Caldwell and keeping house for him?' asked Sandy, and he chuckled appreciatively.

'Exactly, but you have made a plain statement of the facts and would never think of looking beyond those facts, I'm sure. Many people are not happy to do that. They want more meat, the juicier the better. And if they don't find it they make suggestions in the hope of finding out more and, before you know it, a story has been made up which goes the rounds and it eventually becomes accepted as the truth.' Bitterness edged his voice. 'It damaged my father's reputation as much as it did Phillida Caldwell's. But you've left out one story concerning the Caldwells, the one which involved Lymond, supposedly, and was based on a grain of truth.'

'All I know is that he might have been blamed for something his brother did.'

'So you've heard that, have you?' He seemed quite cheered. Maybe there's a chance yet for him to live that one down. He was never a saint by any means, but you're quite right, he was blamed for something that Crawford had done.'

'Could you tell me about it?' she asked diffidently, well aware that she was doing the forbidden—ferreting for information.

'One of the twins became involved with a married

136

woman. Anywhere else it might have gone unnoticed, but here in a small community where they were well known and the woman was the sort who boasted about her affairs, it became the talk of the district. One day she let slip the name of the twin. It was Lymond.'

'Crawford had used his name?' exclaimed Sandy.

'Probably. She wasn't the first they had deceived in that way, you know. My sister suffered from their mischievous tricks too.'

'But all Lymond had to do was deny it.'

'I know. But he didn't. In fact I don't think he was asked to. The actual blackening of his character didn't take place until after it was learned that he had left Duncreggan and had gone to Canada after having a blazing row with his father.'

'Nan told me that Lymond quarrelled with his father over the condition of the estate,' said Sandy.

'And she's probably right. Lymond was always keen on agriculture, and he told me once that it upset him to see the estate deteriorating through lack of good management and farming. He had every right to be upset, because he knew that one day he would inherit it. But the quarrel came at a bad time. Everyone assumed it had been about the affair with May Burgess and that Sir Gavin had heard about it and had blown his top.'

They had reached the driveway to Duncreggan House, and Bill changed gear to turn in between the gateposts.

'How do you know it was Crawford and not Lymond who was involved with May Burgess?' she asked.

'I learned about it a few years ago, quite by accident. I'd been sailing and I called in at the village pub for a pint. Crawford was there and we sat and talked for a while. I was just thinking of leaving when May came in with some friends. We hadn't seen her for ages, because after the affair she and her husband had moved away. She saw Crawford and came across to speak to him. She asked him what he'd been doing since their little "adventure" together. I could see he wasn't at all embarrasssed or surprised, and when she had gone I said to him: "So it was you and not Lymond?" He stared at me for a minute, then laughed. "Gave myself away, didn't I?" he said. "What are you going to do about it? Tell Helen?" '

'Why should he ask you if you were going to tell Helen?' asked Sandy quickly.

'At that time there was the possibility that he and Helen might get married. She was always friendly with the twins, being the same age as they were and meeting them on the beach in much the same way as Lorna and Euan now meet Dermid,' he replied. 'When I didn't answer Crawford, he said, "You can tell her, if you like, and see if I care. An awful lot of water has gone under the bridge since my little affair with May, and I doubt if anyone will believe it was me and not Lymond now." And with that he left the pub.'

'Did you tell Helen?'

'No. I told my mother instead.' Bill put the car in neutral, put on the brake and switched off the engine. Rain rattled on the roof and dripped steadily from the dark green shrubs which crowded about Duncreggan House, gloomy in the grey light of the wet evening. 'Sometimes I wish I hadn't told her,' continued Bill rather morosely. 'She was round here in a flash to see Sir Gavin and tell him in no uncertain terms what she thought of Crawford. Now, he was an eccentric old man. You never knew how he would react, but this touched his pride and his affection for Crawford. It hurt him to learn that his favourite had let Lymond take the blame for something. There was another blazing row. Another son cleared out, but this one vowed never to return and kept that vow. Helen was so upset she went to South America.'

There was something about the way Bill rounded off the story which made Sandy laugh. He sounded as if such temperamental behaviour on the part of people he knew was beyond his understanding.

'Thanks for telling me. I'd better go in now,' she said, aware that the children were getting restive.

'You're welcome. I've done my best during the past few years when anyone has referred to that little affair to point out that it was Crawford who was involved and not Lymond. Now that Lymond has come back and is doing his best to improve Duncreggan I think he deserves a chance. There's been too much gossip about the Caldwells in the past, most of it damaging. Of course in some ways they've asked for it. They don't seem to care what people think of them.'

'Yes, I've noticed that. And Lymond doesn't seem to want anyone to know the truth concerning the affair you've just been talking about. He's still protecting his brother,' said Sandy with a sigh.

'He was, always like that. He always stepped between Crawford and trouble. He was the stronger of the two when they were little, and his mother used to tell him to look after Crawford. It became a habit, I suppose,' replied Bill. He gave her a grave shrewd glance. 'About what my mother said, Sandy, she meant well. She was thinking of your good name and of Martha's. Possibly she was thinking of Helen too. She doesn't want her to be hurt again by a Caldwell.'

'And could Lymond hurt her?'

'He did once before when he went away. She transferred her affections to Crawford and he went away too. Now Lymond is back I think she's hoping they might pick up where they left off. It would be easier for her if there was no more chance of gossip about him.'

'And there will be if I stay?' she queried.

'Yes, I'm afraid so. Perhaps the best thing would be for you to tell Lymond about it. He might take some action then.'

When she went into the house she found that neither Lymond nor Johnnie was in. She assumed they had had their meal and had gone out again. She bathed Dermid, put him to bed and by the time she went downstairs again Johnnie was back and had brought Ron Carson with him.

'I've brought the photographs you were asking for,' said Ron. 'I think you'll find them of interest.'

There were three photographs, enlargements showing different views of the area taken from an aircraft flying below the usual transit altitude so that details could be seen. It was the one taken of the castle, the house and the hill behind it that held Sandy's attention. It showed quite clearly the pattern of Celtic fields, some roughly square, some oblong and some in the shape of a broad diamond under the surface of one of the larger modern fields.

But the area round the castle was disappointing. It showed nothing of the shapes which would be left by earlier buildings. The hill behind the house was a different matter. It showed contours which could be the circular ditches dug round the base of a fort.

Sandy explained what she could see to the two men, and Johnnie exclaimed,

'But to dig out a place like that would take weeks of work. You couldn't do it alone.'

'No, I couldn't. It would take a team of experts, but at least I can find the site and perhaps do a little surface digging. Since there hasn't been much cultivation in that area it's just possible that I might find something. Thanks for bringing the photographs, Ron.'

'Don't mention it. I suppose there's no chance of Lymond baby-sitting his nephew while you come down to Creggan with us this evening? There's another dance.'

'No chance at all. He isn't in.'

'Gone to visit his sister-in-law, perhaps?' said Ron with a twinkle in his eyes. 'You should hear some of the talk going on over the tea cups about who's going to be the next mistress of Duncreggan. Will it be Martha Caldwell or Helen Lindsay? Have you any ideas on the subject?'

'No, I haven't,' she snapped. 'I wish people wouldn't gossip.'

'Might as well tell the world to stop turning,' said Ron, and then gave her a sly assessing glance. 'Of course I've heard also that there's an unknown in the running, a young inexperienced filly . . .'

'Johnnie, take him away before I hit him,' said Sandy, laughing.

'All right, I'm going,' said Ron. 'Pity you can't come tonight. Tell you what we could do, though, on Sunday. We could take wee Dermid for a sail. Tide's full just after one o'clock, so we could set out while it's making, sail out to Westport . . . have a swim there if the weather is fine and come back with the ebb.'

'That sounds lovely,' said Sandy. 'I'll keep my fingers crossed for good weather.'

After they had gone she sat down and studied the photographs again, glad that she had seen the Mote because this helped her to recognise the shape of a similar construction on the site of Duncreggan Hill. If it could be excavated it would prove that Gavin Caldwell had been right and that Duncreggan had been an important place long before the Norman knight Sir Guy Caldwell had been granted the land there.

She wished suddenly that Sir Gavin were alive so that she could tell him, and the desire to share her discovery grew so that she decided to write to Derek Sloan. It was a long letter, and she enjoyed writing it and sharing with him the story of Duncreggan. It brought him back into her life, made her think about him and look forward to meeting him again. It also made her aware that she would not be here for much longer, two or perhaps three weeks more, maybe less if Martha decided to let Dermid go and stay at Brookfield and she was able to go back home.

She didn't want to go home, at least not yet. She wanted to stay here and dig about in the earth, possibly to find some fragments of pottery or even another brooch. She wanted to visit the dungeon in the castle and walk along the tunnel to the shore which had been used by smugglers in the past. And then there was the library to tidy up. Oh, yes, there was a lot she could do at Duncreggan, if only she were allowed to stay.

By the time she had finished writing the letter it was quite late, so she made herself a hot drink and took it up to bed with her, where she sat up for a while reading some more of Sir Gavin's history. She was now in to the part which described the battles which had taken place in the area between the Scots and the English at the time of Robert the Bruce. The Caldwell knight of the time had supported the Scottish King and had been rewarded for his efforts with more land and power. A touch of romance had been introduced when he had become enamoured of the daughter of one of his English prisoners and had eventually married her.

Once again her dreams when she slept were concerned with the now familiar black knight. This time she was running away across the sands at the head of the Firth, trying to reach England, until suddenly and sickeningly she began to sink. She was just about to be engulfed by the soft oozing sand when the knight appeared, caught her by the hair and pulled her back to safety. She awoke hot and perspiring, tangled in bedclothes, and was relieved to see that the rising sun had flushed the sky with rosy pink.

When she took Dermid down to the kitchen for breakfast Lymond was there, dark-browed and withdrawn, and the sight of him recalled the dream, making her wonder why she dreamed so much about him. She felt a new heart-thumping shyness of him which made her want to run from the room.

Telling herself she was behaving no better than some

142

adolescent in the throes of infatuation, Sandy began to chatter about the photographs to him and how she was now sure that at one time there had been a Mote at Duncreggan. He listened, watching the play of expression on her face, his gaze, as ever, dark and devoid of expression.

'So what do you want to do now?' he asked when she paused for breath. 'Dig it out?'

'I don't think I can,' she admitted. 'To excavate a place like that would require highly skilled archaeologists. It would also be very expensive to do properly. I could only work on a team. But if you like I could find out for you who could do it. Once it's known that there's a prehistoric site here I expect you'll have the local archaeological society asking permission to come and survey it with a view to excavating.'

'No.' It came out quite vehemently and she glanced at him quickly. He looked pale and tired, as if he had gone to bed late and had got up early. 'I've no objection to you poking about and doing a little digging, but I don't want strangers tramping about the place, possibly digging up the new plantation of trees on that hill. And you know my feelings about the past. Let it lie buried.'

'Very well.' What could she do but agree? It was his land, but she could not help feeling a little disappointed, and for a few moments there was a stiff silence between them which was broken only by Dermid's mutters as he struggled to spoon up his porridge.

'Mrs Brodie isn't coming this morning,' announced Lymond abruptly. 'Or tomorrow. I suggest you and I go up to Kirkton to do the shopping for next week, have lunch at the hotel and then you can go and visit Martha.'

'Won't you go and see her too?' she asked, and his eyes glinted with amusement as if he remembered the conversation of the previous day.

'I might,' he replied coolly. 'Did you enjoy yourself at

Brookfield yesterday? I imagine you learned quite a lot, one way and another, about the more recent history of the Caldwell family and their feud with the Lindsays. Helen and Ada Lindsay would fill you in on certain details, I'm sure.'

She stared at his pale face, noted the satiric dip to one corner of his mouth and knew this was the moment when she should tell him about Ada's suggestion concerning Dermid and why it had been made. She had a feeling his reaction to it might be violent, so she began cautiously.

'Actually I learned more from Bill when he drove Dermid and me back here,' she said.

He glanced up sharply, his eyes narrowing with suspicion.

'Ferreting again?' he accused.

'No, I wasn't,' she snapped back. 'Not deliberately. He told me about the May Burgess affair, how he found out that it was Crawford who was involved and not you, and how that led indirectly to Crawford quarrelling with your father.'

'Dead ashes,' he remarked harshly. 'See what good it does to rake them over? Bill ought to have kept his mouth shut. Why did he tell you about it?'

'He was trying to explain something his mother said to me as I was leaving.' Sandy paused, bit her lower lip to steady it and added in a low voice, 'It wasn't very pleasant to find that I'm the subject of gossip among the local women.'

He shrugged his shoulders and the satirical curve to his mouth became more pronounced.

'Stay in this house and automatically you become the subject of gossip,' he said. 'What has been said about you?'

'Yesterday Mrs Lindsay had some friends in to afternoon tea. I was introduced to them and all the time I had a feeling that things had been said or were going to be said about me staying in this house while Nan is away. In addition to that, both Helen and Mrs Lindsay suggested to me that I shouldn't stay here if I didn't want to be talked about.'

His eyes flickered with a dangerous light and his mouth thinned.

'I see. I understand now why Bill told you what happened. He'd be pointing out to you what a good job has been done in the past to make the Caldwells appear blacker than they are,' he said. 'And how, as a result, anyone who associates with us gets blackened too.'

'Yes. He said it's too bad you haven't been back in the district long enough to live down the blackening of your own character before this happened,' she said, and Lymond seemed to explode with anger.

'What the hell has it got to do with the Lindsays if Nan is here or not?' he exclaimed. 'It's none of their damned business what goes on in my household or who is invited to stay here by me. Oh, I can guess only too well what went on in Helen's mind yesterday. She saw us kissing the other night and then found us both on the floor of the library yesterday, and because we were alone in the house she immediately leapt to the conclusion that you and I are having a torrid love affair.'

'Something like that.' Sandy tried to speak lightly to join in his mockery of Helen, but failed. Her voice quavered and the pinkness in her cheeks deepened. He noticed and his face darkened ominously. The Caldwell pride and temper, normally well hidden by his cool indifferent attitude, were very much on show this morning.

'Blasted chattering women,' he said tautly. 'They've nothing better to do than tear someone's reputation to pieces. I'm sorry it's happened, Sandy. What did Ada Lindsay suggest you should do about it? I'm sure she'd have some plan of action worked out to get rid of you.' There was a savage irony in his tone which revealed that he had no liking for Ada Lindsay.

'She suggested that Dermid could go and stay at Brookfield while Martha is in hospital. He could be looked after by Miss Dobie, Euan's and Lorna's nanny, and I could go back home. She suggested also that when Martha leaves hospital she should go to Brookfield too, to recuperate. That way Bill could keep an eye on his patient and Martha wouldn't be alone here in this house with you, either.'

He was furious, she could tell by the hot glitter of his eyes and the tightening of the muscles in his face. This was how Sir Gavin had become angry, she thought, and as a result had quarrelled with both his sons. But when Lymond spoke his voice was quiet, slightly ironical.

'That was very magnanimous of her, don't you think?' he said. 'And what did Bill think of the suggestion?'

'He told me to tell you about it. He seemed to think you might take some action which would put a stop to the gossip.'

'Did he, now? And what about you? Do you want to go back to England, to escape from the evil designs on your virtue which everyone seems to think this Black Caldwell has?'

His derision had the effect of putting the whole situation in perspective. Sandy couldn't help smiling.

'I may be interested in the past, but my attitudes belong to this half of the twentieth century,' she retorted. 'I don't believe you have any evil designs on my virtue. But I would leave if I thought it would help stop any further blackening of the name of Caldwell. Still, it really depends on Martha, doesn't it? Dermid is her child and I promised I'd stay and look after him unless some alternative is found.'

Lymond leaned back in his chair. The anger had gone from his face and he looked thoughtful as he gazed at Dermid, who, having noticed that no one was paying the slightest attention to him, was picking up porridge from his bowl and dropping blobs of it on to the floor, then leaning over the side of the high chair to see what had happened to them.

Lymond pushed back his chair and stood up.

'I think I will go and see Martha this afternoon,' he announced brusquely. 'It's time she and I had a straight talk. We've beaten about the bush long enough. Be ready about ten o'clock to go to Kirkton.'

He left the room before Sandy had time to think up an answer or even to drop him a curtsey, she thought to herself with rueful humour as she recognised the authority with which he had spoken. She began to clear the table, wondering whether the suggestion made by Ada Lindsay that Dermid should go to live at Brookfield had done what she and Martha had been unable to do; had pushed Lymond into coming to a decision about the boy's future.

But would any decision he made involve asking Martha to marry him? Considering what he had said yesterday in the library she could not believe that it would. Yet, if he did propose marriage to Martha and she accepted him, it would put an end to all gossip in a way which would hardly please Helen Lindsay.

The weather had improved again, and it was in soft hazy sunshine that they left the house for the drive to Kirkton. As they went down the driveway Sandy looked up at the low craggy hill behind the house, noticing for the first time the plantation of new trees to which Lymond had referred. She was longing to go up there and look for any sign of the trenches which would mark the site of the old hill fort and to dig about in the soil in the hopes of finding sherds or flints which might, on closer inspection, reveal the age of the place, but that would have to wait until another day.

As usual the town was busy with holiday visitors and people who had come in from farms to do their shopping. Lymond went with Sandy to the small supermarket and pushed the trolley basket around. To her surprise he selected most of the items they bought, and he was quick to spot a bargain or a reduction in price. When the groceries had been loaded into the back of the car, they walked up the main street to one of the two hotels. On the way Lymond was greeted by several acquaintances and he stopped to talk to a couple of them while Sandy and Dermid waited nearby. He did not bother to introduce her, even though she was aware that the two men he was talking to were glancing at her out of the corners of their eyes. And she decided it was wise of him not to do so, because that would only draw unnecessary attention to her and possibly give cause for more gossip.

They were not able to escape notice in the hotel, however, and had hardly set foot in the pleasant sunny dining room, which was already three-quarters full of people, when they were pounced upon by a smartly dressed older woman who, as soon as she had spoken to Lymond, turned to Dermid and Sandy and said pleasantly,

'And you must be Crawford's widow and this must be your wee lad.'

Lymond corrected the mistake easily and introduced Sandy as his sister-in-law's cousin to the woman, who was called Mrs Grant.

'Och, yes,' said Mrs Grant. 'I've heard Johnnie Currie and Ron Carson mention you. They were at our house the other night with my daughter. They had hoped to bring you too, but you'd left the dance and they said you'd probably gone back to Duncreggan with Lymond.'

For the life of her Sandy could not have controlled the betraying colour which spread over her face as Mrs Grant eyed her appraisingly. After a few more polite words the woman continued on her way out of the dining room and Lymond urged Dermid and Sandy towards an empty table.

'It's out of such innocent remarks made by people like Johnnie or Ron that rumours are manufactured and consequently characters are blackened. My mother suffered in the same way,' said Lymond with a touch of bitterness as he opened the menu to study it.

'It's awful,' agreed Sandy. 'Isn't there anything we can do about it?'

'Short of standing on the steps of the town hall and

shouting out loud that everyone has made a mistake and we're merely friends and not lovers?' he queried derisively.

'Are we friends?' she countered, feeling her cheeks grow warm again.

'We are being forced into friendship by circumstances,' he scoffed. 'Only you and I know the real truth, and that makes us allies.'

She shivered a little, for his words recalled something Nan had once said about Phillida and Stewart Lindsay being the only ones who had known the truth about their relationship, and they had both been drowned.

'What's the matter?' asked Lymond, who had been watching her.

'I was just thinking about your mother and Stewart Lindsay,' she whispered, and, opening the menu, tried to concentrate on choosing something for Dermid to eat. To her relief the little boy was so delighted at being taken out for a meal in a public place that he was behaving angelically, sitting in the high chair which had been brought for him and looking round at all the other people, his big eyes round and his finger stuck in the corner of his mouth.

'There is something we could do about it,' said Lymond, putting his menu to one side and folding his arms on the table to lean forward so that his quietly spoken words would be heard only by herself. 'It would be a little drastic, but it would confound everyone and put an end to speculative gossip, at least for a while.'

She looked up. His eyes were alight with mischief and the muscle at the corner of his mouth twitched.

'I don't expect you'd agree to it, though,' he added aggravatingly. 'You're not ready yet to take such a step.'

'How can you know I'd agree to it or not if you don't tell me about it?' she challenged.

He looked away at someone beyond her, rubbed a hand across the lower part of his face, looked back at her and said slowly:

'To tell the truth, I'm not sure whether I dare tell you, because you'll either accuse me of hypocrisy or you'll storm out of here in a rage, convinced that you've been insulted.'

'You should be able to tell a friend anything,' she said softly, and it seemed to her that his glance held a warmth which she hadn't noticed before as he gazed at her.

'That's true,' he murmured. 'Well, here goes. I'll put our newly-forged friendship to the test. One sure way of stopping any further damaging gossip about our relationship would be to announce our engagement.'

While Sandy sat in stupefied, staring silence the waitress came to take the order. She was aware of Lymond ordering for herself and Dermid without bothering to consult her, as probably he knew he would get no more than a gasp out of her. The waitress knew him and was chatty, which gave Sandy time to recover her equanimity, so that when the waitress had gone and Lymond said quietly,

'Well? What do you think?' she was able to reply with a good show of coolness,

'As you said, it would be a little drastic.'

'But effective,' he countered.

'Probably.'

'Then you agree to it?' He knew how to push an advantage.

'No, no ... I don't. I can't. It'd hardly be worth it for the few weeks I'm going to be here until Martha is able to get about,' she argued. 'Besides, what would Martha say?'

'I don't much care what she says,' he retorted. 'If she hadn't come here uninvited and then invited you, none of this would have happened,' he added callously.

It hurt, as the truth often does. He was so right. Martha had not shown any consideration for him when she had arrived at Duncreggan uninvited and had stayed uninvited, so why should she expect any consideration in return? But if Martha hadn't invited Sandy, she would not have met him and shared a few moments of moon magic. She might not have found out ever what it was like to be treated as a woman instead of a sexless object, and most important of all, she would not have made a new friend.

'It's just that I think she's hoping you'll ask her to marry you,' she muttered defensively. 'And she might be very upset if you and I become engaged even if it's only for a short time. If you asked her instead of me it would have the same effect, you know.'

The dark eyes held a pitying expression, as if he thought very little of her intelligence.

'I told you yesterday your arithmetic is wrong,' he jeered. 'Lymond isn't the only name which begins with L, and although I agree with you that Martha would like very much to be married again and be fenced around with the security she believes marriage brings with it, she hasn't picked on a Caldwell this time. She's going for comfort and stability rather than romance and notoriety. She's chosen a person who is a different from a Caldwell as it's possible to be, someone with red hair, not black, whose family's escutcheon has not been blotted, a man who is wealthy in his own right and who can well afford to keep a woman like Martha, and whose roof doesn't leak. His surname happens to be Lindsay, which begins with an L, I believe.'

The softly scoffing voice stopped speaking as Sandy absorbed her second shock of the day. The waitress came with the soup and for a few minutes she was busy attending to Dermid, making sure he had the right spoon and that his bib was in place. When she turned back to start on her own soup she had recovered sufficiently to speak quite calmly.

'How do you know it's Bill she wants to marry?'

Black eyes glinted with mockery as he looked up from his soup to answer her.

'I can also put two and two together, but I usually get

four as the answer,' he taunted. 'And I'm also pretty sure that Bill won't ask her to marry him until he knows that Dermid's future is taken care of, and that is why Martha wants me to relieve her of the lad's upbringing. I've been taking my time coming to a decision about it because there didn't seem any urgency. I thought we had all summer, but now the predicament in which you've been placed by local gossip has forced my hand a little.' He paused and his eyes glinted with amusement. I can do nothing less, fair damsel, than come to your rescue again by asking you to agree to the announcement of our engagement.'

Sandy stared at him in bewilderment, her soup forgotten. The sights and sounds of the dining room faded from her consciousness. She saw only the cool black eyes of the Knight of Duncreggan looking at her steadily, a little mockingly, as if he sensed her confusion, and she heard only the echo of his voice repeating the suggestion that they become engaged to be married.

'But I don't want to be engaged to anyone,' she said at last.

'Not even to help Martha achieve what she wants for Dermid and herself?' he argued.

'How would it do that?'

'It would give her time. You could stay on at Duncreggan until the end of the summer without any more gossip. It would be a sop to convention, a way of stopping the talk about us. Only you and I would know the truth.'

His face was alive with mischief and she imagined that this was how he had looked when working out some prank with his brother Crawford.

'And at the end of the summer what would we do? Announce that the engagement is off?' she asked warily.

'I hadn't thought that far ahead,' he replied coolly. 'Look, I'll do a deal with you. If you'll agree to let me spread the word today that we're engaged, I'll agree to let you say the engagement is off the day you leave here. I think that's fair

152

and should give Martha the time she needs, don't you?'

It would only be an announcement to stop gossip, only he and she would know the truth. She must remember that, keep it in the forefront of her mind all the time, along with the reason for doing it, which was to enable her to stay at Duncreggan and mind Dermid until Martha had achieved what she wanted.

'I agree,' she said, and found herself chuckling suddenly. 'I can hardly wait to see Martha's face when we tell her. She's going to be very surprised.'

'So are some other people,' Lymond remarked drily. 'But I'm glad you agree. Now we're really allies.'

CHAPTER SEVEN

WHEN they reached the hospital Lymond said:

'I'd like to talk to Martha alone about Dermid. It should take about fifteen minutes. I suggest you take him into the park for a while. We'll tell her of our engagement when you come in.'

Before Sandy could argue he turned away, hurried up the steps and disappeared through the swing doors. Immediately Dermid began to whine.

'I want to go with Uncle Lymond! I want to see Mummy!'

He didn't stop until he was sitting on a wooden swing in the park, clinging with his chubby hands to the chains which attached it to the iron frame and she was pushing him. Then his moans changed miraculously to shrieks of delight as he swung back and forth.

The air was still fresh from the previous day's rain, and the leaves of sycamores and ash trees which screened the park from the road looked sharp and bright as if someone had touched their green with paint. In the neatly arranged borders huge dahlia blooms blazed with exotic colour, scarlet, orange and bronze. Here and there the pale mauve of Michaelmas daisies and the deeper blue of lobelia provided subtle contrast. From where Sandy was standing she could see a different view of the curving hills which glowed with a purple tint against the pale blue sky, an indication that heather was in full bloom.

It was a lovely day on which to become engaged, thought Sandy, then immediately cancelled the errant thought, reminding herself that her engagement was a sham, a practical joke devised by one of the Caldwell twins, those masters of practical jokes, and it had been devised deliberately to confuse local gossips.

She pushed her hand into the pocket of her jacket and felt the stiffness of an envelope against her fingers. It was her letter to Derek. She had forgotten to post it in the town. What would he think of her present escapade? she wondered. Never in a million years would he understand why it had been considered necessary for her to appear to be engaged to Lymond. But then he would never have to understand because she would never tell him about it. By the time she saw Derek again the summer would be over, and so would her engagement to the Knight of Duncreggan.

Dermid had tired of swinging, so she took him over to the slide, where with several other children he mounted the steps fearlessly and slid down, shrieking as he went. After several turns she managed to persuade him it was time to go and see his mummy, and they made their way back to the hospital.

To Sandy's surprise Martha was alone, although the chair beside her bed where she was resting indicated that Lymond had been there. Her pretty face was still pale and she looked as if she had been crying.

'Hello, love,' she said rather dispiritedly after hugging Dermid.

'Where's Lymond?' asked Sandy anxiously, hoping the little talk with her cousin hadn't developed into a row which had resulted in a flood of tears, making it impossible for him to continue further discussion with Martha.

'He's gone to find Helen. She's still working here,' muttered Martha. Then, suddenly casting restraint aside, she burst out, 'Oh, Sandy, Lymond says he wants Dermid to stay at Duncreggan House until I'm better, but he can't stay there unless you're with him, and I can't see how you can stay there after what she's been saying about you and Lymond.'

'What has she been saying?' asked Sandy, feeling herself grow chilly.

'She's been telling everyone that you and he are living together. She was in here this morning telling me that it was all my fault and that I should never have invited you to Duncreggan. She made the most awful remarks about you—I was terribly upset. I told Lymond what she said—I had to or I'd have burst. He went quite white, looked as if he might do murder at any minute and stalked out saying he was going to find Helen and put an end to it.'

'Has he said anything to you about what he intends to do for Dermid?' asked Sandy.

'No. Oh, Sandy, what are you going to do? I'll understand if you don't want to stay on now, but who's going to look after Dermid if you go?'

'I'm not going,' said Sandy. 'I don't have to. You see, Lymond and I are engaged, so that should put an end to any more gossip.'

Martha's face was funny, she decided. It seemed to have frozen into a mask of goggling surprise. Her mouth was slightly open and her eyes were bulging, and for half a second Sandy regretted the fact that Lymond wasn't there to see her cousin's reaction.

'Well, isn't he a cool one!' exclaimed Martha at last. 'Not a word did he say to me.'

'We were going to tell you together. He wanted to talk to you about Dermid first.'

'I think it's the best news I've heard for ages,' said Martha, her face lighting up, the tears chased away by smiles. 'Have you told your parents yet? I bet Aunty Jane will be pleased. I know she's always encouraged you to have a career and has taken pride in your scholastic achievements, but when I was staying with her and Uncle Tom she confided in me that she hoped you'd marry one day. Have you set the date for the wedding yet?'

'No, no.' Sandy felt as if she was being rushed along by a tide which had no turning. How like Martha to think of a wedding day already, as if she considered getting married to be the most important step anyone could take. 'We've only just decided to be engaged.'

'It solves everything, doesn't it?' said Martha, clapping her hands together in uninhibited delight. 'It means you can stay and no matter what Helen says about you it won't matter. You know, I think she's been jealous all along, first of me and now of you, just because we lived in the same house as Lymond. I suppose you haven't chosen a ring yet?'

'No, we haven't,' said Sandy weakly. And never will, she added to herself, wondering if Lymond had given any thought at all to the complications which were already looming on the horizon as a result of the announcement that they were engaged.

'I hope you'll both be very happy,' smiled Martha, her big eyes filling again with tears as the occasion touched her generous if slightly superficial heart.

'You're not upset, are you? You don't mind it's me and not you?' asked Sandy, anxious again.

'No, I don't mind. There was a time when I thought it would have been ideal if Lymond and I could have married and he could have become Dermid's father, but I soon realised it wouldn't work. He and I have nothing in common, nothing we can talk about. We couldn't ever be close friends, I mean, and it's important to be friends as well as lovers if you want to marry. I learned that the hard way with Crawford.'

'But I thought you were happy with him,' exclaimed Sandy, surprised by this serious confession on the part of her frivolous cousin.

'I was while I was with him. He made life seem very exciting, one long adventure,' sighed Martha. 'But he wanted me only when I was lively and pretty, and able to keep up with him. As you know, it isn't always possible to be like that, and when I felt off colour or down in the dumps, he didn't care. At those times he'd go off in search of other entertainment instead of staying to help me and cheer me up. He didn't love me in the way I wanted to be loved, but I'm hoping I've found someone who will love me in that way.'

'Bill?' queried Sandy softly, and Martha flashed her a surprised glance.

'How do you know?' she exclaimed.

'Lymond told me.'

'But how did he know?'

'He's good at arithmetic,' said Sandy, smiling as she saw Lymond coming down the ward towards the bed.

'Congratulations, brother-in-law,' Martha greeted him gaily. 'You couldn't have chosen a nicer person than Sandy.'

'So you've told her?' he remarked, looking across the bed at Sandy. He was frowning and his eyes looked hot and angry.

'I had to,' she replied defensively. 'She was getting into a state of nerves because you'd said that Dermid could only stay at Duncreggan if I'm there, and she thought I mightn't stay after what's been said about you and me.'

His expression softened slightly and he looked back at Martha.

'I'm glad you think our solution to the problem is a good one,' he said quietly. 'I want you to know, Martha, that

I've decided to take care of Dermid's education for you. It's the least I can do for Crawford's son, and I'm sure that my father would have done the same if he had been alive. Also he's welcome to stay with me at Duncreggan until such time as you have found a permanent home.'

Now Martha's face presented another picture, one of stunned pleasure.

'Oh, Lymond,' she breathed. 'I don't know how to thank you.'

'You can do that easily by telling Bill at the earliest opportunity,' he said coolly.

'How did you guess about Bill and me?' she demanded with one of her prettiest pouts. 'We've tried so hard to keep it to ourselves.'

'The night I was in the pub when you were there with him I watched you, and then later I had a chance to talk to Helen and she told me how Bill's mind was working. Apparently he told her he wanted to marry you to relieve her mind, because she imagined you and I were having an affair.' Lymond's voice was very dry and the curve to his mouth was unpleasant. 'She doesn't trust me, you see, and she believes she has good reason not to.'

'Oh, how silly of her,' said Martha dismissingly. 'Have you told her about your engagement to Sandy?'

'Yes. Just now. It should be all round the district by nightfall.' He glanced at his watch. 'And now I think it's time we left.'

On the way back to Duncreggan Sandy posted her letter to Derek, addressed to his home because she had no other address. She guessed it would be some time before it reached him on the Greek island where he was with the expedition. When they arrived at the house they found Johnnie in the kitchen just finishing his tea. He gave them a mocking underbrowed glance and said,

'You're a couple of sly ones!'

'I gather the news has reached Creggan,' remarked Lymond calmly.

'Brought by Helen, who else,' mocked Johnnie. 'She greeted Bill with it as soon as he stepped ashore after to-day's race. I'd been crewing for him, so I heard it all. But I wish you'd let on. I felt a wee bit of a fool having to admit I knew nothing.'

'We didn't know ourselves until this morning,' countered Lymond, smiling at Sandy as if they shared more than secrets with each other. 'Is that all you have to say, Johnnie?'

'Och, no.' Johnnie's wide grin appeared. 'Congratulations and best wishes to both of you. I think it's a great idea. Ron wasn't far out in his guess yesterday, was he, Sandy? And Mother won't half be excited when she hears about it. She'll be saying she saw it in your teacup. Did she?'

'She told me she could see a dark handsome man in my life,' replied Sandy with a laugh, and then felt her flesh creep a little as she remembered that Nan had also mentioned she could see a tall woman who might cause trouble. How right she had been!

'Are you still coming sailing with us tomorrow?' asked Johnnie.

'I'd like to.' She realised suddenly she wasn't quite as free to go and come as she chose, that it might look odd if she went sailing without Lymond so soon after the announcement of their engagement. She glanced at him, Johnnie intercepted that glance and grinned understandingly.

'Ron is pretty keen on helping the course of true love to run smoothly, so I don't suppose he'd mind if you came too, Lymond. It's time you had a day off from this place, anyway. Why don't you take it tomorrow, by way of celebration?'

'Maybe I will,' said Lymond, smiling again at Sandy, and she felt her heart leap with happiness.

Johnnie was right in his assumption that Ron would

welcome Lymond, and when the little blue boat left its mooring just before noon the next day Lymond was aboard helping to put up the jib as the white mainsail billowed forward, filled by a gentle following breeze. Down the estuary it ran towards the line of white-ruffled water which marked the bar where the estuary joined the Forth.

As usual the process of leaving the land behind had the effect of making Sandy forget problems. With Dermid on her knee she sat in the cockpit, quite happy for once to let others sail the boat and enjoying, much to her own surprise, the congratulatory remarks being made to her about her engagement to Lymond by Sheila Grant and the blonde barmaid from the hotel, whose name was Jane Hardwick and who was actually the hotel proprietor's daughter home on holiday from university.

When they had cleared the bar the sheets were hardened slightly and they reached down the shimmering sunlit Firth, eventually turning to beat into a small sheltered bay where they anchored and went ashore to swim. The sail back was less lively because the wind had abated and they were glad of the small engine which pushed them against the rapidly ebbing tide back to the mooring.

As she and Dermid were rowed ashore by Lymond in the little dinghy, Sandy thought dreamily that it had been one of the best days she had ever known. Immediately an idea erupted from nowhere that it had been like that because Lymond had been with her, and that although he had been quiet he had not been aloof and had treated her with a gentle courtesy she had never seen him show before and which she knew had been noticed by the others.

Yet once they were ashore and back in Duncreggan she didn't see any more of him than she had before they had decided to become engaged. Monday morning came. Mrs Brodie arrived, full of congratulatory remarks and many questions. The day took the same course that days had taken the previous week, and in the afternoon when Dermid took his nap Sandy spent the time studying the aerial photographs again. Eventually she took them out on the hill with her as she tried to make out which of the many hollows in the land were in fact the original defensive ditches which had once surrounded the hill fort.

The next few days took a similar course without her coming to any conclusion about the actual site of the fort. Twice she went to Kirkton to visit Martha, both times with Johnnie because Lymond seemed to be too busy. In fact since the weekend she had seen very little of him, and once or twice she wondered whether Johnnie might notice that for an engaged couple she and Lymond were not very fond of each other's company.

It had been a week of doldrums, she decided, its dullness more noticeable because of the excitement of the previous week. Yet when she saw Martha on the Friday evening and took her some clothing to wear when she was released from hospital the next day, she found her cousin in what she could only describe as a mood of subdued excitement and full of questions about the situation at Duncreggan.

'Everything is fine,' Sandy assured her. 'Nothing has changed except that the library is looking tidier. I'm quite pleased with my efforts to clean it up. If only Lymond could afford some paint I think I could make it look like a good example of an eighteenth-century drawing room.'

'That house needs more than a lick of paint,' scoffed Martha. 'It needs the attention of some good plumbers, plasterers and carpenters. Do you feel happier about staying there now, less guilty about imposing upon Lymond?'

'Yes, of course.' She didn't, but it would never do to let Martha know that. 'Why do you ask?'

'I was just wondering. It's important to me that you do stay just a little while longer, Sandy.' She paused, frowned as if something were worrying her. 'Helen came to see me again today. She said she's decided not to stay in Kirkton after all and go into partnership with Dr Parker. Another opportunity has turned up in Glasgow, she says, a chance to do some research on cancer. She's leaving this weekend with her mother. She's awfully upset. I suppose you can guess why?'

'No,' replied Sandy lightly. 'Can you?'

'She's upset by your engagement to Lymond. She's always hoped, ever since she was a girl, apparently, that one day she would marry either him or Crawford. She was very close to marrying Crawford and then he fell out with his father and ended up marrying me. She's been hoping that if she settled down in Kirkton, close to Lymond, one day her wish would come true.'

Poor Helen, thought Sandy, with a sudden surge of compassion. It was true the woman had made trouble for her in the most unpleasant way by making insinuations about the relationship between Lymond and herself, but it had recoiled on her and now she was reacting to hurt by going away again.

But what would Lymond's reaction be to the news that Helen was leaving? Had he foreseen such a complication when he had decided to make the quixotic gesture of becoming engaged to herself? Would he care? There was no way of guessing how he would react, because he was a law unto himself, unpredictable.

She returned to Duncreggan as she had gone to the hospital, on the back of Johnnie's motor-bike. He dropped her at the gateposts and turned round to go speeding down to Creggan. As she walked slowly up the drive, enjoying the fine evening, Sandy's glance was drawn as always to the craggy hill, and she felt her nerves jump with excitement, for there, clearly delineated by the slant of the setting sun's rays, was the shadow of a ditch. Once again one of the simple methods of field archaeology had come to her aid.

Flinging herself into the house, she went to Lymond's study to make sure he was home and able to listen for the sleeping Dermid should he wake. He was sitting at his desk in the pleasant panelled room which was furnished with graceful old Windsor furniture and didn't look up when she said,

'I'm just going up on the hill for a few minutes. Is that all right?'

She took his grunt to mean it was and left the room. It was the end of the month, so she supposed he was filling out forms and trying to balance accounts, all of which seemed to be an essential part of farm work.

The light was beginning to fade, but she managed to find the ditch she had noticed. Walking along it was difficult because it was overgrown with bracken and brambles. Above it to the left the land rose in a gradual slope, and she guessed that the whole hill had been a fort at one time.

She walked on in the twilight and eventually found herself, as she had expected, on the other side of the hill looking down at the estuary of the river which shone with a faint pewter gleam against the smooth blackness of the mud banks. Above the outline of the hills on the western shore the sky was pale green flushed with orange, and a few stars twinkled with faint light.

Immediately in front of her was a fence of barbed wire which marked the boundary of the Duncreggan estate. On the other side she could see that the land had been cleared ready for building and her ditch seemed to have disappeared. Slanting down the hill, she could just make out the trenches which had been prepared for the laying of drainage pipes.

Drainage pipes! Another rule of simple field archaeology. Whenever pipes are being laid or digging is being done before construction work, take the time to explore those excavations in case something of archaeological value is turned up and exposed. Here on the part of the hill which had been sold to Carson the builder, excavations had already been made. All that she had to do was examine them and hope to find some sherds of pottery or other relics which would prove once and for all that there had been a fort built there.

She would come back tomorrow, she decided, and began to make her way home, following the fence until it ended and she found herself on the path which she and Lymond had followed the night they had returned from the dance in Creggan. Below her the castle shimmered faintly with ghostly light, and she could just make out the movement of someone coming towards her along the path—Lymond.

'I was coming to look for you,' he said as they met face to face. 'Your mother phoned. I said you'd phone back when you returned.'

'Has something happened at home? Did she say?'

'No. You seem a little agitated. Are you expecting something to have happened at home?'

'Well, she might have received Martha's letter mentioning our engagement. I had been thinking I ought to tell Mother about it before she received the news from Martha ... but somehow ...' She broke off and peered up at him. 'I'm afraid it's causing complications which we didn't foresee.'

'You use the word complication in the plural. What others do you know about beside this one?' he asked lightly.

'Helen is leaving. She isn't going to work in Kirkton after all.'

'So what? She's a free agent, always has been.' He sounded as usual cool, indifferent to anyone else's problems.

'She's going because she's hurt. Once again she's been hurt by the behaviour of a Caldwell. Lymond, I'm afraid our engagement has messed things up between you and her.'

He didn't reply at once, but when he did he sounded amused and she wished she could have seen his face.

'Are you?' he replied enigmatically. 'Well, I shouldn't

worry about it if I were you. Does having to tell your mother about us bother you?'

'No, as long as you don't mind . . .'

'I don't mind, and far from making complications I think our engagement has definite advantages,' he replied.

His poised stillness warned her. He was about to swoop again to use the advantage now. Quickly she side-stepped round him and began to lunge forward in a run, but his arm shot out and he caught her, swinging her round easily to face him again, holding her, his hands on her waist ready to tighten should she try to move.

'Not so fast,' he drawled. 'The moon isn't full tonight, but there are enough stars.'

She put her hands against his chest to fend him off. She could feel the beat of his heart beneath one hand through the tough denim of his working shirt.

'Just because we've announced we're engaged you needn't think that has given you the right to make love to me,' she said as coldly as she could.

'But I think it has,' he retorted. 'Kissing and making love are essential parts of being betrothed, so I've been told, and I intend to make the most of that advantage.'

'Well, don't expect me to like it,' she retaliated in one more effort to put him off.

It didn't work, and she felt his mouth hard against hers. Fear that she might respond too fervently and so give herself away lent her strength. She managed to pull free and was off down the hill, running as if some fearful monster were chasing her, yet feeling a contradictory delight in kissing and running, half hoping he would catch her and make her pay forfeit.

Through the farmyard she went and into the house by way of the back door. She had reached the door leading from the kitchen to the hallway when he caught up with her. Rough hands seized her, turned her round and slammed her against the wall beside the door. She had a brief glimpse of his eyes glittering like jet in the electric light, then her mouth was being bruised by his, her breasts were being crushed by his weight and she couldn't move or fight the tide of desire which was rising within her.

'You like it,' he said softly and breathlessly against her cheek. 'And before the night is over I'm going to make you admit you like it.'

He pulled her away from the wall, his arms going round her to hold her closely, and this time his kiss was more gentle, drawing from her the response she wanted to give. Her hands went up to touch his face, to twist in his hair, and nothing else mattered any more as she admitted to herself once again that what he wanted was what she wanted too.

Next morning Sandy overslept for the first time since she had arrived at Duncreggan. She awoke to the touch of fingers on her face and opened her eyes in alarm to see a weird-looking clown-like face close to hers. It was streaked with red lipstick and covered with powder. Two big golden eyes looked out of it.

'Sandy, wake up, 'cos I'm hungry and want my breakfast,' chirped Dermid.

She sat up and gaped at him.

'Whatever have you done to your face?' she exclaimed.

'I used Mummy's stuff,' he answered. 'She puts it on her mouth. Do I look pretty like her?' He held up one of Martha's lipsticks. It was mutilated beyond repair and showed every sign of having been chewed.

'You little imp!' she gasped, not sure whether she should laugh at him or scold him. 'I'd better clean you up before your Uncle Lymond sees you, or he'll have something to say to you!'

The possibility that he might be scolded by Lymond had the desired effect and he went with her willingly to the bathroom to have his face scrubbed clean. On the way back to the nursery Sandy peeped into Martha's room. As she had guessed, it was in chaos. Every drawer in the dressing-table was open and clothing had been strewn about. She glanced down at Dermid, intending to be severe. He looked up at her with big golden eyes and his mouth trembled.

'Don't tell Uncle Lymond,' he quavered.

'All right, but you're a scamp, Dermid Caldwell, there's no mistake about that, just as your daddy and your uncle were before you.'

She decided to leave the tidying of the room until later and went downstairs. The kitchen was deserted because both Johnnie and Lymond were with the animals, and Mrs Brodie didn't come that morning because it was Saturday. Dirty dishes had been piled in the sink, and the porridge in the pan looked as if it had been burned. Quickly Sandy made some fresh tea, found some dried cereal in one of the cupboards and poured it into two bowls for herself and Dermid.

She was just crunching cornflakes when Johnnie came in. He found himself a clean cup and saucer, brought them to the table and helped himself to tea.

'You're late this morning,' he taunted. 'Sorry I broke up that clinch you and Lymond were in last night.'

She might have known he wouldn't let it go by without making some sort of remark.

'That's all right,' she replied as coolly as she could, glad that for once her colouring was under control, 'We were just saying goodnight.'

'Och, come off it, Sandy,' he jeered. 'Think I don't know the difference between a goodnight peck and the real hot stuff? Think I would have been blasted by Lymond for returning too early from the village if it had been what you say? He isn't exactly friendly this morning, either.'

No, he wouldn't be, thought Sandy with a rueful grin, since Johnnie by bursting unannounced into the kitchen the previous night had foiled any intention Lymond had had of making love to her until she had been forced to admit she liked it. Disturbed by Johnnie's entrance, he had released her and she had managed to slip out of the kitchen and up to her room.

Aware that Johnnie was watching her with a rather knowledgeable twinkle in his eyes, she attempted to divert him by telling him about Dermid's mischief of that morning, and it was while he was laughing that the phone rang. Asking him to keep an eye on Dermid for her, she went out into the hall to answer it.

'Sandy?' Her mother's voice was clear in spite of the distance that separated them. 'Why didn't you phone me back last night?'

'Oh, I'm sorry, Mum. It was late when I received the message and I thought you might have gone to bed. Is something wrong? You don't often phone long distance in the daytime.'

'No, but the message I have is rather urgent. We had a visit from a friend of yours, a Derek Sloan.'

'But he's in the Mediterranean!'

'Not any more. He's back. The expedition had to pack up sooner than expected. He got back home early this week and found your letter waiting for him. He seemed terribly excited by it and said he would call to see you on his way to visit a friend of his who works in the archaeology department of the Museum in Glasgow, so I thought I'd better warn you. He should arrive this afternoon some time. He's driving up. It will be all right for him to call, won't it?'

'Yes, I expect so. Mother, have you heard from Martha lately?'

'No, I haven't, nor from you. What's going on up there?'

'I've been intending to write to you or phone you. I . . . I'm engaged.'

'Really, darling? How nice. Anyone we know?'

'No, although you've heard of him—Lymond, Lymond Caldwell, Martha's brother-in-law.'

'Well, that is a surprise. I thought you didn't like him.'

'I didn't, at first.'

Jane Phillips' laughter sounded at once delighted and rather knowing.

'That's the way it often happens,' she said. 'But I think you're very wise to have an engagement. Much better than rushing into marriage as Martha did. It gives you a chance to get to know one another as well as a chance to back out before making too serious a commitment, if you decide later that marriage isn't for you. I must go now, dear. Your father is standing behind me telling how much this call is costing him. He sends his love. I'll be writing, and tell Lymond we'd like to see you both when you can come down this way.'

Sandy replaced the receiver with a long sigh of relief. Thank goodness her mother was one of those calm unflappable people. Returning to the kitchen, she found Johnnie playing some sort of game with Dermid which was making the little boy laugh to the point of hiccups.

'Where's Lymond?' she asked.

'Feeding the pigs,' he replied.

'Stay with Dermid a few more minutes, will you, please? There's something very important I must tell him.'

She dashed out into the farmyard. The day was cloudy and windy with a hint of rain in the soft air. Lymond was just entering the yard carrying two empty buckets. He paused by the door of one of the outbuildings when he saw her and waited for her to come up.

'What's the matter?' he asked.

His face was taut and unsmiling above the turned-up collar of his yellow waterproof jacket. His eyes were black and empty and had dark smudges under them, as if he had slept even less than she had.

'Complications,' she explained. 'My mother phoned again. We're going to have a visitor this afternoon.'

'Is she coming?' His voice lilted with surprise.

'No. A friend of mine.'

169

'Not the one with whom you have mutual interests like arrowheads, pottery sherds, and burial chambers?' he mocked.

'Yes,' she whispered, wondering how he had guessed.

'Wouldn't you know?' he gasped, and leaning against the jamb of the doorway burst out laughing.

'It isn't funny,' she exploded. 'It's very embarrassing.'

Lymond stopped laughing and his face hardened. From under frowning brows his eyes glittered at her like black ice.

'Embarrassing?' he repeated. 'Is that how you find our engagement now?'

'Yes. You see, I don't think Derek is going to understand. It's going to be awfully difficult explaining it to him.'

'You're not thinking of telling him the truth, I hope,' he said curtly.

'No, I wouldn't do that without your agreement, but he's going to wonder why and possibly feel a little hurt, in the same way Helen has been hurt,' she said earnestly.

His face remained taut, unsmiling. Only the narrowing of his eyes showed he was giving some thought to what she had just said.

'Did you tell your mother about us?' he asked.

'Yes, I did.'

'Did she understand?'

'Yes, she did. She said we were very wise to have an engagement, that it would give us time to get to know one another and a chance to back out of the arrangement if we find we don't want to marry after all.'

'Then I suggest you tell Derek that when he comes,' he said coolly. 'And if he doesn't understand, it's his hard luck. Now get back to the house to do the job you came here to do and which our sham engagement is enabling you to continue to do . . .'

'But I . . .'

'I've told you what to do. That's what you came out here for, isn't it? Advice. Perhaps you were thinking I would let you become disengaged very conveniently while your friend is here. Sorry I can't oblige. To do it so soon would only cause more unpleasant talk and make it difficult for you to stay on. Sorry too you find it embarrassing, but remember why we decided to do it—to protect your good name, prevent further blackening of mine and to give Martha time. Now excuse me, I'm busy. I have animals to feed.'

He spoke roughly, with that touch of natural arrogance which always made Sandy feel like a serf who owed him fealty, all the time looking at her as if she were some object which disgusted him.

'Yes . . . . *sir*,' she said with a touch of impish humour, and bent her knees in a mock curtesy, but there was nothing impish in her feelings as she turned back to the house. In fact, for the first time in years, tears were brimming in her eyes. She searched for the cause and rejected it at once. Not for anything was she going to admit that Lymond's rough words had hurt her more than they should because she had fallen in love with him.

It was just before noon that the phone rang again. In the middle of preparing the midday meal Sandy answered it, and was surprised to hear Martha's voice at the other end of the line.

'Guess what, Sandy?' she said, her voice full of laughter.

'What?'

'Bill and I have just been married by special licence!'

'But why didn't you tell me last night? You must have known,' protested Sandy.

'Because we wanted to keep it a secret. Will you tell Lymond for us, please?'

'Yes, I will, but won't you be coming here this afternoon as arranged?'

'No. We're going away for a few days to a place in the

171

country that Bill knows. When we come back we'll take Dermid with us to Brookfield.'

'I've never heard of anyone getting married with their leg in plaster or on crutches before,' said Sandy.

'Neither have I,' said Martha with a giggle. 'But we decided we might as well be together since Bill has to treat me anyway.'

Sandy told Lymond and Johnnie the news while they were eating dinner. Lymond made no comment but Johnnie was amazed.

'Och, I don't know what to think. Engagements and marriages all over the place. I'd better move out, back to university before I catch the disease. You know, Lymond, this place hasn't been the same since Martha set foot in it.'

'Hasn't it? Well, don't worry. Everything will return to normal in a week or so,' replied Lymond drily. Sandy felt the shock of his cool black glance and guessed he was referring to the fact that within a week's time there would be no longer any reason for her to stay at Duncreggan.

The thought lingered with her as she spent Dermid's hour of rest in the library, searching again for the artefacts which Sir Gavin had found. She shouldn't really be surprised by Lymond's attitude. He wasn't being any different from usual, coolly indifferent, slightly aloof as if he had decided he didn't want to be her friend any more, as if they weren't allies.

But last night, if Johnnie hadn't come in when he had ... Her thoughts swerved violently away from what might have happened. It was just as well he had, she admonished herself, in the same way it had been a good thing when Helen had interrupted them. If Johnnie hadn't come she would have been added to the flowers which Lymond Caldwell had picked and had thrown away, for she knew deep down inside she coudn't have resisted him for long.

Tears welled in her eyes as she looked down at the book she had just taken down from the shelf to dust. It was big and deep, bound in thick embossed red leather. She lifted the cover and felt a thrill of surprise shoot through her, for it wasn't a book at all but a box disguised as one, and it contained something which had been carefully wrapped in tissue paper.

Tears forgotten, she unfolded the tissue paper carefully and there in her hand lay a perfect example of a penannular brooch, a circle of dull, darkened metal (which could be gold) to which was attached a straight pin for fastening some article of clothing either at the neckline or at the shoulder.

Attached to the brooch was a small card with some words written on it in the writing which she recognised as being Gavin Caldwell's.

'Dug this up on the hill. Confirms the theory put out by Childe at the beginning of the century that at one time Duncreggan was the site of a Dark Age fort.'

Quickly Sandy searched through the box and found in the rest of the paper some fragments of clay which had also been labelled by that surprisingly meticulous man.

'Found this near ditch on the hill. Could be remains of moulds used in metalwork.'

Sandy examined the pieces of clay carefully, wishing she could show them to someone she knew who would recognise them. Then she remembered that Derek would be arriving soon and would be as excited as she was by the sight of them. She replaced them and the brooch carefully in the box, which she put on the desk.

The photograph of Gavin Caldwell and his wife caught her eyes. She picked it up and carried it to the window to see it better. What a strange man he must have been, a mixture of pride and arrogance, deep sensitivity and scholarliness, who had won medals for bravery in action, not for killing but for saving the lives of men who had been under his command.

Her glance strayed to Phillida, noting the puckish humour

in the lovely face. She had heard the woman called a minx, a livewire, an enthusiast who never gave any thought to herself, who had been the only person to volunteer to help Stewart Lindsay sail his new boat and who had been drowned as a result. There was no doubt in anyone's mind that Gavin Caldwell had loved her dearly. But what about her? Had she loved him? Or had she loved Stewart Lindsay? As Nan had once said, only Phillida had known the truth, and she was dead.

Sandy's mind wandered to Bill and Helen Lindsay, the children of Stewart Lindsay. She compared them with Lymond, the only surviving child of Gavin and Phillida, and as she replaced the photograph on the desk her eyes lingered on the dark-haired, dark-browned man whose eyes even in the photograph seemed to glitter like jet, and she murmured to herself,

'If it had been me I know which one I would have loved.'

CHAPTER EIGHT

DEREK did not arrive that afternoon as Sandy had expected, but the next morning—just as she was leaving the house with Dermid, determined to make the most of the returning sunshine by taking the child down to the beach.

As he unwound his lean length from the little black car he was driving, Derek grinned at her and said,

'Hi. What's all this about a Dark Ages fort?'

'You got my letter?'

'Yes. It arrived home the day I did.'

Apart from a tan which the Mediterranean sun had given his long thin face, and a new bleaching of his fair wispy hair, he was just the same, untidily dressed, intense, his blue-grey eyes keen and observant behind his spectacles.

But the sight of him did not make her pulses race, or set any bells ringing in her ears. He was just Derek whom she had known for years and who was more interested in the fort than he was in her.

While her mind was accepting this fact she was answering his rapid questions and taking him into the house to the library to show him her most recent finds.

'The aerial photographs show a definite ditch,' she explained. 'But it's been difficult to make sure exactly where it is, the hill is so overgrown with bracken.'

'I'd like to see the photographs,' he interrupted excitedly. 'I'm on my way to see Noel MacCuish, you know, the chap who was at the dig at Wroxeter. He's working in the Museum at Glasgow just now, and I know he's going to be very very interested in this find of yours.'

'I'll have to ask Lymond if you can take them,' she demurred.

'Who's he?' he asked sharply.

'He's the present owner of the estate, the son of the man who dug these up. He and I are engaged.' It was out at last, and she waited tensely for his reaction.

Derek went on turning the brooch in his hands.

'What do you want to be engaged for?' he asked. 'Doesn't sound like you, Sandy. I thought you'd be impatient of such a convention and want to go the whole way immediately.'

'It's so that we can get used to each other, find out if we want to be married. We could change our minds,' she explained.

'I suppose so. You know there always has been knowledge of a sixth-century fort hereabouts.' Now he was turning one of the pieces of clay over and over in his hands, obviously more interested in what it might represent than in her engagement to Lymond. 'But this looks like a piece of a clay mould for an ornament. Look, it has an interlace pattern marked on it. Reminds me of some of the moulds we've picked up from excavations of Anglo-Saxon settlements. And this piece has a runic inscription . . .'

He didn't care about the engagement. It meant nothing to him. For him she was only a person with whom he could discuss mutual interests like pieces of pottery or penannular brooches. He did not see her as a woman and would never see her as one.

'I'm going to phone Noel,' he announced suddenly, replacing the finds in their box. 'I'm going to ask him to come and meet me here. Is there anywhere I could stay? A bed and breakfast place?'

'In the village, I expect. Johnnie will know. But I should warn you, Derek, Lymond won't let anyone excavate on this side of the hill, on his land. He's planted new trees.'

'That's a nuisance.'

'But last night I followed what I believe to be the ditch and found it goes right round the hill. It ended on a building site where they're digging trenches for drains.'

He looked up at that, interest glinting.

'Drains, eh? Better and better. Do you know the builder?'

'I know his son. He found the aerial photographs for me.'

'Good. How soon can we go there?'

'Now, if you don't mind my bringing Dermid.'

Creggan looked soft and serene in the morning sunlight. The tide was in and a few boats were drifting about the placid water of the estuary, but fortunately Johnnie and Ron were still on shore. They welcomed Derek with their usual geniality, and in no time had him fixed up for bed and breakfast in one of the local houses. Then they all went up the hill to examine the trenches dug for drains.

Time passed quickly up there on the sunny hillside and it was with surprise Sandy realised that it was well past twelve. Ron obligingly drove her back to Duncreggan, and just as they were turning into the drive they had to stop to let a small blue car out on to the road; a car which Sandy had no difficulty in recognising as belonging to Helen Lindsay. She had a glimpse of Helen's haughty profile as the car went past on its way, not to Brookfield but to Kirkton.

There was no sign of Lymond in the house, so she prepared Dermid's meal and gave it to him, had a light lunch herself, put him to bed for his rest and spent the next hour in the library at her self-appointed task of cleaning it up. When Dermid awoke, she took him with her up the hill. He complained about the long walk, but forgot his complaints when he was allowed to help her and Derek dig about in the mud at the bottom of the trenches made for the drains.

Although they found nothing of interest that day, Derek was very hopeful. He had managed to phone his friend Noel, who would be arriving the next day, and towards the end of the afternoon he walked with Sandy back to Duncreggan with the intention of asking Lymond's permission to show Noel the artefacts Sandy had found.

They found Lymond in the farmyard tinkering about with the engine of one of the tractors which was again in need of repair. He acknowledged Derek with a cool nod of his head and went with them into the house to see the brooch and the pieces of clay.

'Would you mind if Noel took them away to Glasgow to be authenticated?' asked Sandy.

'No. As long as you don't start digging on my side of the hill I don't mind what you do,' he replied indifferently.

'If anything is proved, credit will be given to your father's work, naturally,' said Derek enthusiastically. 'Sandy has been telling me about the history he wrote. I hope you'll get it published.'

'I might,' replied Lymond at his most laconic. 'I hope you'll give some credit to Sandy too—for ferreting.'

'Of course we will. She's going to be helping with the digging during the next week. Carson, the builder, is willing to hold up any further work until we've made a thorough examination of the site.'

'Good.' Lymond sounded as if he didn't care one way or

the other, and he went from the room without excusing himself, without even glancing at her.

'I don't get it,' said Derek, suddenly. 'I just don't get it.'

'What do you mean?' she exclaimed.

'You and him,' he said challengingly, turning to face her as if to surprise admission out of her.

She nearly told him. It nearly all came pouring out, how the engagement was a pretence to put paid to gossip. Only the realisation that he wouldn't understand, no matter how much she explained, stopped her.

'Maybe my ideas about such things are all wrong, but I imagined you'd be a bit more lovey-dovey with each other,' Derek continued rather diffidently, as if it embarrassed him to discuss such a subject as love between two people.

'How do you know we aren't?' she countered spiritedly. 'When there's no one else about? Our feelings about each other are ours alone. They don't have to be put on show for the entertainment of others.'

'I suppose you're right,' he admitted. 'I think I'll get back to the village. Ron Carson has invited me to his parents' home for a meal.'

His remarks about her relationship with Lymond lingered with Sandy irritatingly for the rest of the day and most of the next few days, as Lymond's withdrawal became more and more marked. Often it seemed to her that she was back in those first two weeks at Duncreggan when she had seen him only at mealtimes. It was as if she had shared nothing with him, least of all their secret concerning their engagement.

Taking Dermid with her, she spent as much time as she could on the other side of the hill. Noel MacCuish had duly arrived and had decided to stay for the week, and with him and Derek she dug diligently yet gently with her trowel in the drainage trenches, finding several objects of interest, including a piece of polished bone which could have been the handle of a comb and which had part of a name inscribed upon it, as well as several more pieces of clay moulds. There were, however, some flints of an earlier period that puzzled Noel, but it wasn't until Derek came across a bank of stones and earth which looked as if it had once formed the rampart that he decided that an excavation on a larger scale would have to take place to ascertain exactly the age of the fort.

'That could take about five or six weeks,' he said. 'I'm going back to the Museum to see if anything can be done about it, because Carson says he's in no hurry to build the houses here. He has plenty of other work he can do. He was just preparing the site for some speculative building in case anyone came along wanting a new house in the area. I'd like to thank you two for alerting me about the place, though. It's a pity you won't be here for the final dig, Derek.'

'Well, I have to get back to Dulchester to fix up about my research. I'm not sure what Sandy is going to do now,' replied Derek.

Neither was Sandy, but the problem was solved for her that very evening with the return of Martha and Bill, who called in at Duncreggan on their way to Brookfield to pick up Dermid. Lymond was out and had been in Kirkcudbright all day at a meeting.

Although she was still on crutches Martha looked radiant and Bill was his usual humorous self.

'You can come and stay at Brookfield, if you like,' Martha said to her cousin. 'Until you and Lymond set the date, although I expect you'll want to go to Hampshire before you do that, won't you?'

'Yes, I'll want to go to Hampshire,' said Sandy. 'I could go with Derek. He's leaving this afternoon.' She noticed the puzzlement on Martha's face and explained quickly what had happened concerning the fort.

'It's very exciting,' she finished rather lamely, aware that her cousin was bored by the whole thing.

'Possibly,' agreed Martha. 'Anyway, let me know what you're going to do, and tell Lymond we're back and would like to see him. The details of what he plans to do for Dermid are still to be worked out, you know.'

They left, and Sandy wandered back into the house. It was strange to be without Dermid, to be free to leave if she wanted. But she wasn't really free. She had to wait for Lymond to tell him that Martha was back, so there was no need for her to stay any longer and they could now break off their engagement.

The trouble was she didn't want to leave. Even the prospect of going to Dulchester and arranging to take a postgraduate degree no longer tempted her. Up the stairs she went to her room, intending to pack her rucksack so that she would be ready when Derek called, as he said he would, on his way to Kirkton and the road which led south. She packed in a desultory way, trying to keep her mind a blank, pushing all sorts of disturbing thoughts about Lymond away from her because they had a tendency to hurt too much.

But they kept springing back to mock her, and with them came her own glib words about love and about hoping to know by the end of the summer whether she had found someone she wanted to marry and live with.

Well, the end of the summer had almost come and she knew she had found someone to love, a friend whom she wanted to live with always, in any way that he decided, she didn't care as long as she could stay with him, be near him so that they could argue and taunt together, walk in the moonlight together, laugh and love together.

When she had finished packing she went to the window and leaned there for a while. The day was grey, and a strong wind from the south-west was blowing, sending the clouds scurrying across the sky and whipping the water of the Firth into crests of white foam. An errant gleam of pale sunlight slanted down between the clouds. It touched the grey walls of the castle so that they shimmered.

'The splendour falls on castle walls.' The line from a poem by Tennyson leapt into her mind, and all at once she was swept back in time and was seeing the castle as it must have appeared in the Middle Ages, splendid in its strength. In the courtyard knights in armour had gathered, sunlight struck sparks from shining lances, and gay, colourful pennants fluttered in the breeze. But one knight sat his black charger a little apart from the rest, elegant in grey and black, a plume of black feathers in his helmet, and it seemed to Sandy he looked up at a window in the castle where a lady stood.

She blinked and came back to reality, remembered the dream she had experienced the first night she had slept in that room; the dream which recurred time and time again and which she shared with the black knight of Duncreggan. She had never been down to the cellar of the castle to find the dungeon, and if she didn't go now she would never see it.

She went from the room, skipped down the stairs and into the kitchen. Johnnie was there, having just come in from the barn.

'Where would I find the key to the castle?' she asked him.

'It's hanging on a nail in the porch. It's a Yale lock. Why do you want it?'

She explained quickly, told him that Martha had called and had taken Dermid to Brookfield, and then ran from the house, ignoring his call to be careful while she was in the castle.

As she struggled against the wind on her way to the castle, Sandy noticed that the leaves of the trees were already touched with autumn gold and that the hedge bulging over the walls that edged the path was bright with the red of hips and haws. Clusters of orange berries swung from the rowan trees that swayed in the wind beside the castle, a sure sign that summer was on the wane and would soon be over.

She had no trouble in opening the door. Inside the old cars looked the same, possibly a little dustier. In the corner of the room the trapdoor in the floor, which led to the cellar, was open as if someone had been down there recently.

She went down the wooden ladder carefully, pleased to find that the cellar had been wired with electricity and that whoever had been down there had left the light on. The underground room was cool and a little damp, but it was clean and obviously used as a storage place. Rough wooden racks had been built to store cans of machine oil and parts of engines.

In one corner was the dungeon, a small cell built from blocks of stone. It still had a door with an iron grille in it. She peeped through the grille and shuddered a little at the thought of being locked up in such a small dark place.

Set into the wall adjacent to the dungeon was a solid wooden door studded with iron nails. She lifted the latch of it, pulled it open and found a tunnel yawning blackly in front of her. Pleased to have found the smuggler's tunnel so easily, she stepped into it and groped her way along the damp walls by the light which filtered into it from the cellar. Her exploring fingers touched another door which had been set into the rock fairly recently, judging by its design, and had been fitted with a Yale lock which could be opened from the inside without a key. She assumed it had been put there to prevent casual walkers on the shore from entering the castle by the way of the cellar.

She turned the knob of the lock, pulled the door back and found herself facing a ridge of sand beyond which the wind-tormented waters of the Firth hurled themselves in fury at the land. The wind lifted her hair and set it swirling about her face as she stepped on to the shore and looked about to see if it were possible to walk from this point, either to the estuary of the river or to the horseshoe bay where she had played so often with Dermid. Neither way looked very tempting, for sandbanks gleamed sleek and slippery with the water which lashed over them, and she remembered Lymond's warning that the sands in the area were treacherous.

She was just thinking of returning to the castle when she heard a thudding sound. Hurrying back, she found the door had closed, slammed possibly by some contrary draught of wind created by the opening of doors in the cellar. At once her hand went to the pocket of her anorak to take out the Yale key which she was sure would fit this lock as it had fitted the other. But there was no key in her pocket, and she remembered ruefully that she had left it in the lock of the castle door.

This time she was locked out, not locked in, and her situation was distinctly dangerous. If she were any judge of the tide, it was on the flood and from the look of the shore it would come right up to the door, covering the narrow ridge of sand on which she was standing. The only way out of her predicament looked dangerous too. She could risk being sucked into the sands or she could risk breaking her neck by trying to climb the sheer slant of rock on which the castle was built.

She was looking up at the rock, wondering where she might find footholds and handholds, when there came the sound of the door being opened. It swung back and there in the opening, elegant in a grey suit worn with a black turtlenecked shirt, stood Lymond.

Hands on hips, he looked at her with cool blank eyes, his face as still as if it had been carved in pale stone. Hands in the pockets of her anorak, her bright hair streaming sideways in the wind, her grey eyes wary, Sandy faced him, the calmness of her attitude betraying nothing of the sudden excited beating of her heart.

'I believe this is the seventh time I've rescued you, if you count our engagement as one. It could be lucky,' he remarked drily. Then, his face stiffening, he added more severely, 'Next time you go through this door be sure to have the key with you.' He held out a hand and showed her the key he had taken from the door upstairs. Hiding a desire to fling herself into his arms and thank him for coming to rescue her again, Sandy stepped past him into the tunnel and said coolly,

'There won't be a next time. I'm leaving Duncreggan today, that's why I came to see the dungeon. Martha and Bill returned this afternoon and they took Dermid to Brookfield with them, so there's no need for me to stay any longer. I'll go with Derek.'

He closed the door and they were in the damp-smelling semi-darkness of the tunnel, so close together that she could hear him breathing, feel his warmth. She turned quickly and hurried into the cellar. To be close to him and not touch him was more than she could bear just now, when parting from him was so near in time.

'Do you want to go?' he asked as he entered the cellar behind her and closed the door.

'I have to get back to make arrangements to return to university,' she replied dully. 'To find out if I've been accepted to take a further degree.'

'So you still want to do that more than anything else?' he persisted. 'I thought that maybe you'd want to stay and be a member of the team which is going to do the excavation on the other side of the hill.'

She turned to look at him. He was leaning against the door and watching her with narrowed eyes.

'I would like to, only . . .' She broke off, biting her lip, clenching her hands in her pockets, her eyes glistening with the tears she refused to shed in case he thought she was like Martha and given to pouring out floods of tears when she couldn't get what she wanted.

'Only what?' he prompted.

'It would be easier for us to break off our engagement if I left, wouldn't it?' she muttered, looking down at the floor so that he could not see those tears.

'I suppose it would,' he agreed indifferently. 'Do you want to break it off?'

Her head came up sharply. The tears had gone and she could see him clearly. His face was taut and unsmiling, his eyes were dark and empty.

'That was what we arranged to do,' she replied.

'I know it was,' he said, and stepped towards her suddenly. She moved backwards and found herself against the door of the dungeon.

'Supposing I tell you I don't want you to leave, that I'm seriously thinking of locking you up in the castle so that you can't leave,' he said softly, coming closer to her, and now his eyes glittered like jet. 'Oh, I'd feed you. I'd bring you meat and wine, and after we'd eaten and drunk we'd make love and before the night is over you'd be admitting that you like it,' he added tauntingly.

'Lymond!' she gasped. He had come very close and had placed his hands flat against the wall on either side of her so that she was trapped. 'You talk beautiful nonsense. You weave enchanting fantasies, but I can't stay.'

'I didn't ask you if you *could* stay, I asked if you *want* to stay. There is a difference, you know,' he retorted. 'You're welcome to stay, if you want to, not just until summer is over but for as long as you wish.'

'Would there be any conditions?' she countered in a whisper, scarcely believing that he meant what he was saying.

'One. You'd have to marry me. Do you think you could bring yourself to take such a step? To come down off that high intellectual perch of yours and condescend to marry a rather impecunious landowner whose outlook on life is decidedly earthy and whose family name has a few nasty blots on it? If you would, I'd try not to give you any reason to regret it.'

His nearness was beginning to torment her again. She was longing with every part of her for him to kiss her and sweep her into passion, and the desire was making it difficult for her to think clearly and logically.

'Do I have to give you an answer now?' she evaded.

'Yes, or be locked up.' He said it quite seriously without a flicker of a smile.

'Oh, how can I give you an answer when I don't know how you feel about me?' she argued rather shakily. 'This week you've been so offhand and withdrawn that I began to think you would be glad when I could leave and the engagement could be over so that you and Helen could pick up your relationship where it left off. I saw her leaving here last Sunday and I thought you must have told her the truth . . .'

Lymond's hands were on her shoulders and he was shaking her to make her stop.

'Your arithmetic is appalling,' he scoffed. 'No one knows the truth about our mock engagement and no one ever will know, if I can help it. Helen came to see me before going to Glasgow to tell me she was sorry for the trouble she had caused. If you had been there I'm sure she would have apologised to you too. And as for picking up any relationship she and I might have had, that was all on her side. She imagined she had one with me, although most of the time I lived here with Crawford, she didn't know the difference between us.' His voice quivered a little with laughter as he remembered past mischief.

'Then why have you ignored me all week, ever since she left?' Sandy asked.

'Because I thought I wasn't wanted once your fellow historian turned up. Because I thought I was an embarrassment to you. I'm not as prickly as my father or Crawford used to be, but I have my own share of Caldwell pride. I didn't like being regarded as an embarrassment by you. But now your friend has gone and you're still here.'

'Gone? Derek has gone? When did he go?' she exclaimed.

'He was leaving as I arrived home. He was taking Johnnie into Kirkton. Johnnie told me you were here in the castle, so I offered to come and fetch you so that you could say goodbye to Derek. But he said he couldn't wait. He'd promised to be in Carlisle this evening, for some reason, and wanted to be on his way. He said he supposed you wouldn't be back at Dulchester in October and that he understood why. It was then that I realised I had another chance, which must be seized at once without hesitation. Now what's it to be, fair damsel? The dungeon? Or surrender to a force which we both feel and which is stronger than we are?'

Sandy was still not sure how he felt about her. For him it might only be a physical force and have nothing to do with the spiritual union which she had always dreamed true love should be. After all, he had just admitted that his outlook on life was decidedly earthy, and she knew all about the Caldwells being hot-blooded.

But, as he had guessed, the force was as strong in her as it was in him. It was stronger than both of them, this urge to be together, to stay together no matter what differences lay between them, and so maybe it was right to give into it.

'Surrender!' she cried, going willingly into his arms which held her closely and strongly as if he had no intention of letting her go.

'Any conditions?' he murmured eventually against her hair.

'There's only one.'

'What is it?'

'If I tell you I want to marry you because I love you, you're not to think I'm using the word love to cover my self-interest,' she said very seriously.

He pushed her away from him, holding her at arm's

length so that he could see her face, and although his eyes were as black as coal without a flicker of light in them, the tell-tale muscle twitched at the corner of his mouth, so that she knew he was amused by her condition.

'I promise I won't think that,' he replied, 'because it's just possible I'll be using that much-abused word love myself very shortly in the hope that your reaction to it will be much in my interest. But I'd like to be out of here and in the comparative comfort of the house before I talk of love to you.'

Taking her hand he led her towards the ladder, but at the foot of it she turned to him, still uncertain, half afraid it was a dream she was having.

'Really?' she whispered.

Now his eyes held that warmth which she had seen in them once before, a glow—could it be of tenderness?

'You're very hard to convince,' he scoffed gently. 'Perhaps if I put it this way you'll believe me. You are the only flower I've wanted to pick and keep. You are the only woman I've ever asked to marry me. I don't know of any other way to show you the depths of my feeling for you except by asking you to marry me. Now you've stayed in my house for a while and you know a little about me. Do you think I would ask you if I didn't feel more for you than for any other woman I've known?'

'It isn't that I don't believe you, Lymond,' she replied. 'It's just that I can't believe it's happening to me. Why me?'

'Because you're the only woman who has ever shown you care about what I'm doing with this place, because you're not interested in titles, position or money, because you need convincing all the time that you're not a sexless object, because you need rescuing every so often. Oh, there are lots of reasons why I want to keep you here and love you. But who wants reasons? I don't. All I want is you here at Duncreggan with me, and if you won't stay I'll have to lock you up so that you can't get away. I know that what I have to offer isn't much in comparison with a research degree or a career in archaeology, but it's all I have and . . .'

Her fingers pressed against his mouth stopped the flow of words as she cried out,

'Oh, Lymond, please, it's more than enough. I only want what you want, and it's been that way for some time.'

'Then let's get out of this damp hole, and I think when we're in the house you'll find I won't object to you telling me you love me, or showing me either.'

They kissed briefly, and there was a wealth of promise in the sweet simple gesture. Then Sandy turned and went up the ladder, her heart singing with joy because her dream had merged with reality and she was going to stay with the black knight of Duncreggan for ever.

Send coupon today for
FREE
Harlequin Presents
Catalog

We'll send you by return mail a complete listing of all the wonderful Harlequin Presents novels still in stock.

Here's your chance to catch up on all the delightful reading you may have missed because the books are no longer available at your favorite booksellers.

Fill in this handy order form and mail it today.

Harlequin Reader Service
MPO Box 707,
Niagara Falls. N.Y. 14302

In Canada:
Stratford, Ontario
N5A 6W4

Please send me without obligation my FREE Harlequin Presents Catalog.

NAME _____
(please print)

ADDRESS _____

CITY _____

STATE/PROV _____ ZIP/POSTAL CODE _____

Complete and mail this coupon today!

YOU'LL LOVE
Harlequin
Magazine

for women who enjoy reading fascinating stories of exciting romance in exotic places

SUBSCRIBE NOW!